"Are you all right? Did something happen?"

"Nothing's wrong." She turned away. Nothing, except that her pulse was racing from what she'd just seen.

"Why are you out here?"

He stopped beside her. She felt the heat from his body and knew he was close.

"I just…"

She glanced back at him, and that one tiny glimpse drew her uncontrollably. His hair was ruffled. Whiskers darkened his chin. He'd closed the center button on his shirt, but that was all. The tail flapped in the breeze. The cuffs were open. Black crinkly hair covered his chest. His broad, bare chest.

"What are you doing out here?" Stephen asked.

Never—ever—in her entire life, in all the countries she'd lived, in all the circumstances she'd found herself, had Caroline once wanted to press her hands against a man's chest. *Until now….*

Dear Reader,

This month our exciting medieval series KNIGHTS OF THE BLACK ROSE continues with *The Rogue* by Ana Seymour, a secret baby story in which rogue knight Nicholas Hendry finds his one true love. Judith Stacy returns with *Written in the Heart,* the delightful tale of an uptight California businessman who hires a marriage-shy female handwriting analyst to solve some of his company's capers. In *Angel of the Knight,* a medieval novel by Diana Hall, a carefree warrior falls deeply in love with his betrothed, and does all he can to free her from a family curse. Talented newcomer Mary Burton brings us *A Bride for McCain,* about a mining millionaire who enters a marriage of convenience with the town's schoolteacher.

For the next three months, we are going to be asking readers to let us know what you are looking for from Harlequin Historicals. We hope you'll participate by sending your ideas to us at:

Harlequin Historicals
300 E. 42nd St.
New York, NY 10017

Q. What are your favorite historical settings?

_____
_____

Q. Which Harlequin Historicals authors do you read?

_____
_____

Whatever your taste in reading, you'll be sure to find a romantic journey back to the past between the covers of a Harlequin Historicals novel. We hope you'll join us next month, too!

Sincerely,

Tracy Farrell,
Senior Editor

JUDITH STACY

Written In The Heart

Anne,
Good
luck with
your writing
See ...
Judith Stacy

HARLEQUIN®

ISBN 0-373-29100-0

WRITTEN IN THE HEART

This edition published by arrangement with Harlequin Books S.A.

® and TM are trademarks of the publisher. Trademarks indicated with
® are registered in the United States Patent and Trademark Office, the
Canadian Trade Marks Office and in other countries.

Visit us at www.romance.net

Printed in U.S.A.

Please address questions and book requests to:
Harlequin Reader Service
U.S.: 3010 Walden Ave., P.O. Box 1325, Buffalo, NY 14269
Canadian: P.O. Box 609, Fort Erie, Ont. L2A 5X3

To Judy and Stacy—thanks for always listening
To David—thanks for always being there

Chapter One

Los Angeles, California
April 26, 1896

Surely there was an easier way for a woman to get work.

Caroline Sommerfield shifted on the leather seat of the hansom cab, mentally rehearsing the speech she'd prepared. She'd waited weeks for this chance. She wasn't about to waste it. Even if it meant sneaking around and lying about her whereabouts tonight.

"Who is it you're visiting, Caroline?"

Across the darkened hansom Caroline heard her cousin's voice. She hadn't wanted Sophie to come along with her tonight. But since they'd both been leaving their aunt's at the same time she couldn't reasonably protest.

"A friend," Caroline said. "A sick friend."

"I didn't realize you knew anyone in the city but family," Sophie said.

"I've met a few others," Caroline said.

Sophie was quiet, so Caroline figured she'd accepted her lie as fact. Which was good, because Caroline wasn't particularly adept at telling less than the truth, even to someone she hardly knew, like her cousin.

"How did you meet this friend?" Sophie asked.

Caroline cleared her throat. "All those parties Aunt Eleanor arranged invitations for."

"Really? Which party?"

"Last Saturday night's."

"And whose was that?"

Caroline tightened her grip on her handbag to keep from wrapping her hands around her cousin's neck. This thing of having family, of answering to other people, was getting on her nerves. It was all so strange. And inconvenient.

Still, Caroline had no one but herself to blame for her uncomfortable circumstances tonight. This wasn't what her father had had in mind when he insisted she travel to Los Angeles and move in with her aunt a month ago.

"The Latham party," Caroline said. "We met there."

"Oh, yes, the Lathams," Sophie said. "That's where you showed off your—what is that *thing* again?"

The *thing* that had nearly sent Aunt Eleanor into a faint.

"Graphology," Caroline said. She'd repeated the word dozens of times since arriving in Los Angeles.

"Oh, yes. Quite...interesting," Sophie said. "Aunt Eleanor was..."

"Surprised?"

Sophie managed a polite laugh. "Yes, something like that."

Despite Aunt Eleanor's embarrassment, Caroline had been the hit of the party. The craft of analyzing handwriting was a novelty here, but Caroline had studied it from masters in France and Germany, where the skill was taken more seriously. After only a few minutes of studying a handwriting sample Caroline could interpret the character of the writer. Only a few people in this part of the world could do that.

"Did your father know about your...talent?" Sophie asked.

"Of course," Caroline said. "He encouraged me."

Caroline wished her father were here with her now. Instead he was happy and contented in Europe—where Caroline wished she were—while she'd been exiled to the States.

To find a husband, of all things.

She'd been annoyed with him for weeks but now she just missed him. He meant well. After all, at twenty-four years of age Caroline was more than old enough to be married. That's why she'd agreed to come, why she hadn't protested this husband-hunting expedition, why she let Aunt Eleanor parade her from party to party.

Besides, Aunt Eleanor wasn't as smart as her father and didn't know her as well, so she wouldn't catch on to Caroline's real intentions until it was too late. She didn't want or need a husband. She had plans of her own.

Caroline gazed out the window of the hansom, forced to admit that those plans weren't turning out as well as she'd like. She'd been a little surprised by the reception she'd gotten two weeks ago at the Pinkerton Detective Agency—even after she'd dropped her father's name.

They recognized Jacob Jackson Sommerfield as the renowned detective on the Continent, the man who'd solved some of Europe's most intricate, puzzling crimes. But how, exactly, did that apply to his daughter?

No one at the Pinkerton Detective Agency knew what a graphologist was. She'd explained it, presented her references, even offered a demonstration, but they simply weren't interested.

Undaunted, Caroline had trotted out her skills at all the parties she'd attended these last weeks. Parlor tricks were hardly what Caroline had intended when she'd studied the craft, but it looked as if they had finally paid off. She'd been approached by a Mr. Richard Paxton on behalf of his employer, who had offered her a job. A real job.

The clip-clop of the horses' hooves ceased and the hansom swayed to a stop. Sophie peered out the window. The glow of the streetlamps reflected on her face and Caroline saw her eyebrows bob.

"Good gracious, Caroline, you didn't tell me your friend was *rich*."

"Rich?" She leaned closer to the window.

"Yes, rich. This is West Adams Boulevard. It's become as famous as San Francisco's Nob Hill and New York's Fifth Avenue. Haven't you heard of this place before?"

She'd heard. The elite of the nation had considered Los Angeles a vacation spot, then moved here permanently once they'd recognized the area's potential wealth. These affluent people built their mansions in the West Adams district, setting standards and creating the finest homes found in the city.

"Goodness," Sophie said. "Just look at this house."

Caroline gazed out the hansom at the beveled and stained glass windows of the magnificent three-story house. It was a huge square brownstone with circular turrets on each corner. Palms, shrubs and hedges flourished behind a scrolled wrought-iron and stone fence.

When Richard Paxton had instructed her to meet with his employer at his home tonight, she'd had no idea the man was wealthy—at least, not this wealthy.

Visions of an aging, cranky old man came to Caroline's mind. A curmudgeon too set in his ways to see her during normal business hours, in his office.

"Oh, and look, Caroline. They're having a party," Sophie said.

The house was lit from top to bottom. Faint music

drifted out into the street. Dancers glided past the glowing windows on the second floor. On the balcony a man in a tuxedo stood with a woman in an exquisite gown.

"Are you properly dressed?" Sophie asked, concern in her voice.

Caroline looked down at her blue dress. It was the height of fashion, since her father provided a generous allowance, but far from appropriate for a party on West Adams Boulevard.

Caroline reined in her panicky thoughts. "I'm here for a jo—to see a sick friend, not attend the party."

Sophie nodded. "Well, I suppose..."

"Don't tell Aunt Eleanor about this," Caroline said. "I wouldn't want her to get the wrong idea."

"I see your point." Sophie smiled. "All right, I won't say a word."

Carrying her small satchel Caroline climbed out of the hansom, paid the driver and stood on the walkway until the cab moved on. It irked her a bit that Richard Paxton had put her in this position—or rather, that *his employer* had put her in this position.

But a job was a job. Mr. Paxton had assured her that she was just what his employer needed. He'd been adamant.

So who knew where tonight's meeting might lead? Caroline squared her shoulders. She didn't care. As long as it wasn't marriage.

* * *

He considered shooting himself in the foot, just as an excuse to leave his own party.

Stephen Monterey watched his elegantly attired guests dancing in the ballroom under the half-dozen crystal chandeliers, laughing, sipping champagne. They were having a wonderful time, or as good a time as polite society allowed itself to have. His aunt Delfina would be pleased. Apparently Stephen was the only one who was bored.

Or the only one who had important matters waiting for him.

The face of Russell Pickette sprang into Stephen's mind, making him angry all over again. Damn that Pickette. The lying son of a bitch had brought a halt to a profitable business deal. He'd brought up old memories, too, ones Stephen couldn't quite shake.

Stephen glanced at the mantel clock, anxious for his birthday party to conclude, the guests to leave, things to get back to normal. Turning thirty-two was nothing to celebrate. Just another day. Certainly not worth the time it took to dress in a tuxedo, suffer through a formal dinner, open gifts he didn't want, attempt to make small talk with guests he hardly knew.

"Stephen? Stephen, dear?"

His aunt chugged toward him, her face drawn in its perpetual lines of worry. She wore the maroon gown he'd had to help her pick out, the diamond tiara he'd assured her wasn't *too much*, the elbow-length gloves that hid the rolls of flesh on her arms.

"Stephen." Breathless, she latched on to his elbow. "The party, Stephen, the party. I just don't *know*...."

"What's wrong, Aunt Delfi?"

"I'm not sure if it's going well. I'm not sure at all." Delfina touched her hand to her large bosom. "I think...I think my knees are feeling numb."

"Your knees are fine, Aunt Delfi." Stephen patted the fingers digging into his arm. "The party is wonderful."

"Wonderful?" Panic widened her eyes. "Only *wonderful?*"

"Perfect," Stephen said. "The party is perfect."

She pressed her lips together. "Oh, it's so difficult to plan properly. Your uncle Colin always did this sort of thing, you know."

Stephen simply nodded. Of course he knew. His uncle, Delfina's brother, had run the house, the business, the family—everything—until he'd passed away last winter.

Stephen took her hand and gave it a gentle squeeze. "Everything is perfect. Everyone is having a perfectly wonderful time."

Delfina gazed hopefully over the sea of guests. "Oh, do you think so?"

"I'm certain."

"But you?" Delfina looked up at him, fresh worry lines creasing her forehead. "Why aren't you dancing? I invited several young women for you—"

"I'm enjoying myself." Stephen managed to smile. "Having a fantastic time."

He eased her toward the crowd. "You should see to the guests, Aunt Delfi."

"Oh, of course. Oh dear, oh dear..." Delfina blended into the swarm of guests again.

Stephen made his way to an empty corner, watching the dancers but thinking about the work that waited on his desk downstairs. A suite of offices had been built into the house, from which the business was run. His uncle had liked being at home. Though never married, he'd pulled together an assortment of relatives—Stephen included—and made them his family.

Uncle Colin had taught Stephen everything he knew, and Stephen had taken over the operation of their vast holdings long before his uncle had become sick. Since his death, Stephen had stepped in to fill his uncle's role in every aspect of the household they all shared.

Leaning against the wall, Stephen slipped his hand into his pocket and pulled out a folded note card. So far, it was the only interesting thing about the evening.

It was from Richard Paxton, his assistant, his friend. Richard wasn't at the party but was expected shortly.

According to the note, Richard's birthday gift to Stephen would arrive sometime during the party. And it was just what Stephen needed.

Stephen smiled and slipped the note in his pocket again. *Just what he needed.* What could that mean?

He thought back over the conversations he and

Richard had shared recently. Business. They always discussed business. Stephen didn't remember mentioning anything he needed, because he didn't need anything.

Leave it to Richard to liven up his birthday party with this cryptic message. He'd known Stephen wasn't looking forward to the party his aunt had insisted upon; she'd been concerned about the family's social position since Uncle Colin's death.

Stephen pressed his lips together, thinking harder. The only conversation they'd had recently that stood out in his mind and didn't involve business was when Richard came late to work one morning a few weeks ago. Richard was never late. But he'd been at the wharf at San Pedro the night before, checking on a cargo shipment, and had met a beautiful young woman who turned out to be a prostitute.

According to Richard, being late for work that day was well worth it. He'd been so dazed by the woman that he'd bumped into furniture all morning long. Richard had raved about her and said that Stephen should—

Heat ignited low in his belly, fanning through him like wildfire. He tensed.

Was that Richard's gift? The woman?

Stephen looked around at his guests. These were wealthy, dignified people, as close as Los Angeles came to aristocracy. Surely Richard wouldn't send him a whore for his birthday, right under the noses of his guests—and his aunt.

Even if it was *just what he needed.*

No, Richard must have something else in mind. But what? He knew Stephen didn't need anything, didn't want anything.

Still, Stephen couldn't let go of the idea. His imagination started to roam. A slow heat built inside him. He bit into his lower lip to keep from smiling. Would Richard do such a thing?

Richard wasn't like his other friends, these people in the ballroom. He'd give Stephen something he really wanted—really needed.

A smile bloomed on Stephen's face. Yes, he just might do it.

"Excuse me, sir."

Jarred from his thoughts, Stephen found Charles, their balding butler, standing at his elbow.

"A visitor has arrived, sir."

Another guest. The last thing he needed.

"Send him up, Charles."

The butler shook his head. "Not an invited guest, sir. A personal visitor, she says."

"*She?*"

"Yes, sir. Sent by Mr. Paxton."

"Paxton?"

"Yes, sir." Charles frowned distastefully. "I explained to the young woman that you were occupied, but she insisted—"

"No, that's fine, Charles. I'll see to her myself."

Stephen hurried out of the ballroom, anticipation humming in his veins. Could this be his present from Richard? Would he have actually done such a thing?

At the top of the steps, Stephen stopped. The

first meeting

grand, central staircase led straight down to the marble foyer and the carved, double front doors. Off to the right he glimpsed a woman wandering through the sitting room. Was this she? His gift?

The woman turned and Stephen's knees weakened. Oh, yes. Beautiful. Shapely. A woman meant for rolling around in bed with, if ever he'd seen one.

Just what he needed.

Stephen trotted down the stairs and across the foyer. He forced himself to stop at the entrance to the sitting room.

"Good evening," he said.

She swirled. "Mr. Monterey?"

Heavens, she was pretty. Not gorgeous, but touchable. Wholesome and natural-looking. With big blue eyes framed by dark lashes, soft skin, full pink lips, brown hair.

She had on one of those shirtwaist dresses that Aunt Delfi thought so scandalous, with a bell-shaped skirt pulled across the front and gathered high in back, emphasizing her small waist. High buttoned shoes peeked out from under the hem. Her bosom filled out the pleated blouse; a big soft bow was at her throat. Large leg-of-mutton sleeves on her short jacket made her wrists look small.

And that hat. Stephen loved the wide brim, all done up with ribbons and flowers, dipping over her face at a provocative angle.

Not what he expected to see in a whore. She looked more like one of the ladies Aunt Delfi invited to tea. But he hadn't seen a whore in a while, and

Richard had said he'd mistaken the woman himself, at first.

Stephen stepped farther into the room. "I'm so glad you're here."

She heaved a little sigh of relief. "Oh, thank goodness. You were expecting my arrival."

"Anticipating is more the word."

"I'm Caroline Sommerfield. Mr. Paxton asked me to come here tonight."

"So Richard did send you?"

"Yes, he did."

"For me?"

She frowned slightly and clutched the handle of her satchel tighter. "He said I was to speak to you specifically. But when I saw that you're entertaining guests, I thought that maybe—"

"Oh, no, that's fine." Stephen couldn't hold back his grin. "Actually, it's perfect."

"Well, then." Caroline cleared her throat. "I suppose we should...proceed."

A full smile broke over his face. "Let's not waste a minute."

"Mr. Paxton said you have an office here in your home. Should we go there, or did you have some other place in mind?"

His office. Oh, heavens. Right there on the desk. Stephen thought his knees would give out completely.

He gestured grandly toward the foyer. "My office, by all means."

Caroline hesitated a moment. "Mr. Paxton said

he would be joining us. Should we wait? After all, he did recommend me after seeing my demonstration at a party."

Stephen frowned. "You gave Richard a...demonstration? At a party?"

She shook her head. "Just a sampling."

His heart thudded harder. "Richard is on his own, as far as I'm concerned."

She held up her satchel. "I brought references."

His eyes widened. "References?"

"Yes, and my tools."

"Tools?"

"Oh, yes. I've found that one needs tools to do a thorough job," Caroline said. "You do expect a thorough job, don't you?"

Stephen opened his mouth, but no words came out, just stutters and some babbling. All he could manage to do was point.

Music from the ballroom upstairs drifted down as he led the way to the suite of offices at the back of the house. Halfway there he realized he was walking so fast he'd left her behind. He stopped and waited for her.

Caroline hesitated as he opened his office door and hurried in ahead of her. Only a few lights burned in this part of the house. It was quiet, except for the music. No one else was around. Cautiously, she peered into the office. Stephen Monterey moved briskly about the room, clearing off his desk.

He looked around suddenly, realizing that she was

still in the hallway. He hurried to the door, looking stricken.

"You haven't changed your mind, have you?" he asked.

Caroline glanced around. The situation was a little unnerving, but this was the opportunity she'd waited for. She wanted the job.

"No," Caroline said. "I haven't changed my mind."

She drew a deep breath and walked inside.

Chapter Two

He wasn't what she expected.

From the way Richard Paxton had spoken about his employer, Caroline had pictured an eccentric old geezer. Not the handsome Stephen Monterey.

He was over six feet tall, she estimated, since her nose was about level with his shoulder. He had black hair. Green eyes with little worry lines crinkling the corners. He looked dapper in white tie and tails, and a single-breasted vest. It made his shoulders look straight and his chest wide.

And maybe he was a little eccentric, Caroline decided, since he was clearing off his desk for no apparent reason, hurriedly piling everything onto the floor. But other than that he seemed intelligent, capable of running the large international business Mr. Paxton had mentioned.

Stephen scooped up the last stack of papers from the desk and dropped them on the floor. He ran his hand slowly over the walnut finish.

"You don't mind if we do it…here, do you?" he asked.

Caroline bit into her lower lip. "Are you unwell, Mr. Monterey? You look flushed. Feverish."

"Anxious to get started, that's all." He dashed past her and closed the office door. "Key. I need the key."

He hurried back to his desk and began pawing through the drawers.

Caroline took a step away. "I'd prefer you didn't lock the door."

He looked up. "But someone might walk in."

She glanced around. "So?"

He sank forward, bracing himself on the desktop, and drew in a huge breath. He let it out slowly. "Miss Sommerfield, you're one hell of a woman."

All right, she'd never been on a job interview before, but this was decidedly strange. She wished Mr. Paxton would arrive.

Caroline dropped her satchel onto the desk, anxious to get this over with. During the hansom ride over she'd been thrilled at the prospect of securing a job. In the sitting room she'd been a little intimidated by the opulence of the house, a home well beyond that of her aunt Eleanor. Now Caroline sensed a spark in the air, radiating from Stephen. It caused something to flicker within herself, and unnerve her.

Across the desk, Stephen straightened. "You may as well get…comfortable."

"Comfortable?" Caroline asked.

"Yes." He nodded quickly. "Do you need anything?"

A cup of tea, laced with a shot of brandy, suddenly seemed appealing.

"No, let's proceed," Caroline said. "Where would you like to start?"

He circled the desk and looked her up and down, taking his time in doing so. His gaze traveled from the tips of her shoes to her skirt, to her face, to her hat.

Caroline flushed. Her skin tingled beneath her dress. A heat flowed from him, wafting over her.

Finally he nodded. "Your dress," he said softly. "Take it off."

Breath left her lungs in a frightful huff. Caroline froze to the floor, staring at him. Had she heard him right? Had he told her to undress?

"But wear the hat," Stephen said. "And your shoes."

Indignant outrage surged through Caroline, stiffening her arms at her sides. "I will do no such thing."

"Oh." He looked disappointed. "All right, then take everything off."

Her mouth flew open. "How dare you suggest such a thing?"

Stephen stepped closer. "You'd prefer I undressed you myself?"

"I can't believe you have the gall to speak to me that way!" She faced him squarely, too angry to back away. "How could you say such a thing?"

He spread his arms. "Because you're a whore."

Caroline slapped him—an openhanded, round-house swing that landed against his cheek so hard it knocked him back a step.

"You bastard! You shameless, conniving bastard!" Caroline trembled with outrage.

Stephen pressed his fingers against his cheek. "If you think I'll pay you extra for the rough stuff—"

"Shut your filthy mouth!" Caroline yanked her satchel off the desk. "You horrible, disgusting man! You lured me here pretending—"

"*Lured* you? Richard Paxton arranged this—"

"So, you're *both* in on it."

"I'm not *in* on anything," Stephen insisted.

The office door opened and Richard Paxton walked into the room. Caroline saw him and her anger turned to rage.

"You!"

She drew back her hand and slapped his face, just as hard as she'd slapped Stephen. Stunned, he plastered his palm to his cheek, staring at her, completely lost.

"You're both disgusting," Caroline said. Anger, humiliation, hurt coursed through her as she backed toward the door. "I hope you two are proud of yourselves. Tricking me. Luring me here with empty promises. Making me think I could really have a—a…"

She burst into tears. Big, gut-wrenching sobs. Both men stared, holding their cheeks. Caroline pressed her palm to her lips and ran out the door.

They just stood there for a few seconds, staring at the empty space Caroline had occupied. Finally, Stephen turned away.

"Great birthday present," he grumbled. "Thanks a whole hell of a lot."

Bewildered, Richard held out his hands. "What did you do to her?"

"Does it look like I had time to do anything?" he demanded. He stalked back to his desk. "Next year just send me a box of handkerchiefs."

"You can't let her leave," Richard said. "You need her."

Stephen knelt, gathering ledgers into his arms. "The next time you decide to send me a whore, make it one that will—"

"A *whore?* She's not a whore."

Stephen stopped. He glanced up. "She's not?"

"No. Where did you get that idea?"

"From you."

"Me?"

Stephen fished the folded note card from his pocket. He thrust it at Richard.

"See? Right there. Your gift was *just what I need.*"

Richard looked at the note. "Just what you need to prove Pickette is a fraud."

"What?" Stephen shot to his feet, dumping his ledgers onto the floor.

"Caroline Sommerfield is a graphologist. A handwriting expert. She can prove that Pickette's document was forged."

Stephen gnashed his teeth together, spitting out curses. "Why didn't you tell me that in the note?"

"Because it was your present. I wanted it to be a surprise."

Stephen cursed again. "Go get her back."

"Oh, no." Richard held up his hands and backed away. "I'm not getting slapped again. You made this mess, you'll have to deal with it."

"Damn…" Stephen paced back and forth, rubbing the back of his neck. He stopped. "Are you sure she's a—what is she?"

"A graphologist. And yes, I'm sure. I saw her at a party last Saturday and her skills are unbelievable. One look at someone's handwriting and she can size up their personality in a snap. She can compare samples and tell who wrote what." Richard shook his head. "I'm telling you, Stephen, she can prove Russell Pickette forged that document."

Stephen cursed again and ran out of the office.

Damn this city.

Caroline stumbled down the street, sniffling, wiping away tears, hopelessly lost. She had no idea where she was, no idea which way was home.

Home.

A wave of fresh tears spilled down her cheeks. Home was with her father, not here in this dreadful place. Even though she'd been born in America, as had her parents, they'd migrated to Europe when she was just a child. The Continent had been her home ever since.

Caroline gulped back a sob, willing herself to calm down. She couldn't think while crying. She deserved to cry, no doubt about it. But right now she needed to get to her aunt's house, and for that she needed to think.

Instead, the vision of Stephen Monterey leaped into her mind. He'd intended to have his way with her tonight, deflower her. Right there on his desk. Wearing only her hat and shoes.

Caroline's cheeks burned at the thought, spreading a strange heat through her. She'd been kissed before, and she knew about men and such. After all, she'd lived in France for quite a while. But no man had ever suggested making love to her—certainly not on a desktop. It was scandalous. Outrageous.

Intriguing and a little titillating.

Caroline's cheeks burned hotter. What had Stephen intended to wear?

She gasped aloud at her unladylike thought and the mental image it conjured up. Stephen was a big man. If the whispered gossip she'd heard were true, that meant he—

Caroline pinched the bridge of her nose, forbidding herself to think any further. At least on the subject of Stephen Monterey. Right now she had pressing problems to deal with.

She looked around the neighborhood at all the beautiful homes and knew she was still on West Adams Boulevard. She hadn't gotten very far. A block or two, maybe. She wasn't sure. She couldn't measure distance well through tear-blurred eyes.

Drawing in a fresh breath, Caroline considered her options. She could approach one of the houses and ask for directions. That, surely, would raise questions about why a woman was alone on the streets at this late hour. She'd already been mistaken for a prostitute once tonight and didn't want to go through that again.

If she knew where a police station was she could go there. They could take her home. But what would Aunt Eleanor say when she arrived under police escort? Caroline wasn't anxious to explain her circumstances to anyone, particularly her aunt.

Well, she had to do something. She gazed up and down the street in both directions. Maybe if she—

A man appeared under a streetlamp down the block. Caroline's breath caught. Good gracious, it was that Stephen Monterey. He'd come after her.

Caroline hitched up her satchel and took off.

Running footsteps sounded on the pavement behind her, spurring her to move faster. She heard his voice shouting.

Her high buttoned shoes and whalebone corset didn't make the best athletic attire, and her satchel dragged like an anchor, bumping against her thigh. But she couldn't face that man. Not after what had happened at his house, and certainly not so soon after the thoughts she'd just been entertaining about him.

"Stop, Miss Sommerfield."

He appeared at her side, jogging along with her. Caroline's heart jumped into her throat.

"Go away!"

"No, wait. Stop."

"Leave me alone!" Breathless, she hugged her free hand to her stomach. She could hardly keep going.

"Just stop," he said. "Please."

She slowed simply because she couldn't take another step. Stephen stopped, too, and it annoyed her that he wasn't even breathing hard, while she was panting like a steam engine.

"What do you want?" she demanded.

"I came to see if you still wanted the job."

"Oh! Of all the nerve!" Caroline headed off down the street again.

"And—" he blocked her path "—and to…apologize."

Caroline put her nose in the air and turned her head away.

"Look, Miss Sommerfield, I was misinformed about your…purpose for coming to my home tonight," Stephen said. "Richard told me you were just what I needed, so when I saw you I thought—"

"—that I looked like a common streetwalker?" Caroline tossed her head. "Well, thank you very much."

She whirled away and started off again.

Stephen caught up with her and put himself in front of her, forcing her to stop.

"No, that is not what I thought," he said. "It's just that it's been a long time since I—"

Stephen curled his hand into a fist and pressed it

against his forehead. "Let me start again. You see, Miss Sommerfield—"

"Oh, never mind." Caroline dropped her satchel, finally catching her breath. "It's my fault, anyway. Not yours."

"Your fault?"

"Yes, mine. Mine, for trusting Mr. Paxton. For being foolish enough to come to your house at night. For thinking you were an upstanding, decent businessman." Caroline nodded emphatically. "Believe me, I will not make *any* of those mistakes again."

Stephen pushed his fingers through his hair, watching her, obviously holding in words that itched to be spoken. Finally, he said, "Regardless of all that's happened, Miss Sommerfield, I am in need of a— What are you again?"

"A graphologist."

He waved expansively. "The position is still available. Are you interested in discussing it?"

Her eyes widened. "You expect me to work for you? Now? After all that's happened?"

"Richard thinks you're good at what you do," Stephen told her. "But, frankly, that remains to be seen."

"You won't find a better graphologist than me," Caroline said.

He doubted he'd find a graphologist at all, actually. But he didn't want to go hunting for one. Not when he had this one standing in front of him, who was exactly what he needed.

"Well, are you interested or not?" he asked.

Caroline pressed her lips together, thinking. Was she being a fool twice in the same night to even consider going back to his house?

Here in the soft light of the streetlamps, Stephen Monterey didn't look so intimidating. The breeze had blown his hair over his forehead and his chase after her had disheveled his tuxedo.

He had apologized. Mix-ups happened; she understood that.

And she did need the job. Aunt Eleanor had more parties, teas and dinners scheduled, more eligible bachelors to parade her in front of. If one of them actually took an interest in her she'd never fulfill her dream of working for the Pinkerton Detective Agency.

"I don't have all night to stand around out here, Miss Sommerfield. Are you interested in discussing the job or not?"

There was something dangerous about Stephen Monterey. Not because of what had nearly happened at his house just now. She wasn't frightened of him, not in a physical sense. If he'd wanted to hurt her, or force himself on her, he'd had opportunity to do so in his office, and there was nothing to stop him from taking what he wanted at this moment.

No, the danger in Stephen Monterey was something deeper. Something that could seep into her soul. Caroline couldn't put a name to it. But it tugged at her, nibbled at her already, though she'd only just met him.

"All right, look," Stephen said. "Come back to the house. We'll discuss the position there."

Caroline shook her head. "No, I don't think I should."

She felt his stare bore into her, and she could see he was displeased that she'd turned him down so easily. Stephen Monterey was a man used to getting his way.

"You can't stand out here on the street all night." The tiniest hint of a smile twisted his lips. "Somebody might get the wrong idea."

She couldn't argue with that. Even if Stephen went on his way and left her here, she still needed to get back to Aunt Eleanor's.

"Come back to the house," Stephen said again. "I'll have my driver take you home."

She'd be wiser to leave now, at this moment. To walk the streets until dawn, if that's what it took to get home—and away from this man.

They gazed at each other in the dim light of the streetlamp, until Caroline felt herself being drawn to him so intensely it startled her.

But Stephen broke eye contact first and shuffled his feet. "Well, Miss Sommerfield?"

"All right," she finally said. "I'll come to your house for a ride home. But nothing more. No talk of hats and shoes and…desktops."

Stephen pulled in a quick breath and looked pained for a second or two. Then he grabbed up her satchel and held it in front of him.

"Certainly. Go ahead, Miss Sommerfield. I'll follow you."

Chapter Three

She found Richard Paxton pacing the office when she returned to the house, with Stephen maintaining a discreet distance behind her.

"Miss Sommerfield, I'm terribly sorry about what happened," Richard said, coming forward.

He was a pleasant-looking man, nearly as tall as Stephen and close to the same age. He had dark hair, and blue eyes that at the moment reflected the sincerity in his words.

"I'm to blame," Richard said. "I didn't make clear to Stephen exactly what my gift was."

"Gift?" Caroline looked back and forth between the two men.

"Yes," Richard said. "Today is Stephen's birthday."

"Your birthday?" She turned to him.

"Yes, and so far it's been a hell of a disappointment," Stephen grumbled. "Miss Sommerfield is going home. I instructed Charles to have the carriage brought around for her."

Caroline stood across the room from the two men as an awkward silence enveloped them all. She willed herself not to look at Stephen, but her gaze darted his way just the same. He watched her. Studied her, actually, like a cat waiting at a mouse hole.

"Can I offer you some refreshment?" Richard asked.

"No, thank you," Caroline replied.

Another silence stretched in the office. Stephen began pacing behind his desk. She tried to ignore him. In fact, she wanted desperately to ignore him, but he kept looking at her, making her uncomfortable.

After a few moments he stopped.

"You may as well go ahead and show me what this graphology is all about, Miss Sommerfield," Stephen said. "You're already here and have to wait for the carriage, anyway."

It was a reasonable suggestion and, in a way, she was almost relieved to have something to focus on, rather than endure Stephen's stares.

"Well, all right," Caroline said. "I guess I may as well."

Richard picked up her satchel, which Stephen had left by the door. "Where would you like to work, Miss Sommerfield? The desk?"

Caroline's gaze collided with Stephen's.

"No!" they said in unison.

Stephen groaned softly and sank into a wing chair in the corner.

"How about this table?" Richard suggested.

He led her to a round table with four chairs in the

corner opposite Stephen. Caroline assembled her tools—several magnifying glasses, straightedges, papers and pencils—while Richard fetched several handwriting samples from a cabinet.

"You can use these, Miss Sommerfield." He presented them to her and smiled. "Can I get you anything else?"

She glanced past him to Stephen fidgeting in the chair. He crossed one leg, then the other, then the first again.

"No, thank you, Mr. Paxton," she said.

"Is there any way I can make you more comfortable?" Richard asked.

The question brought Stephen's gaze around to Caroline, his face drawn in tight lines. Only a few minutes ago he had offered to make her more comfortable by undressing her.

Caroline refused to let herself blush, and deliberately turned back to the papers spread out in front of her.

"I'm fine," she lied.

"All right, then." Richard smiled. "Just take your time. There's no rush."

It was more than a little unnerving being in Stephen's office again. Caroline wasn't sure she could concentrate. A strange sensation vibrated through her, stirring her senses to a sharper awareness, making everything seem more intense.

She glanced across the room once more and found Stephen staring at her again. He looked away sharply. Caroline drew in a calming breath. She got out her magnifying glass and went to work.

Faint strains of music drifted from upstairs and a clock ticked somewhere in the house, then chimed the hour. Caroline lost herself in her work, as she usually did.

She wasn't so absorbed, though, that she didn't notice Stephen every time he moved. He seemed agitated. He squirmed in his chair, then paced, then sat again. Beside him in the matching wing back, Richard read a stack of papers, oblivious to them both.

Caroline worked steadily, and when she was finished she looked over her notes one final time, then rose from her chair.

"All done?" Richard asked, coming to where she stood, smiling at her again.

He was a nice man and Caroline felt at ease with him. Like a brother, she guessed, though she didn't actually have a brother to compare him to. But Richard had been equally pleasant at last Saturday's party where she'd met him, and so far, he'd been the only amiable thing about tonight. She was sorry she'd slapped him.

"Yes, all done," she said.

"Maybe you could tell Stephen a little about graphology?" Richard suggested.

He was in the chair now, his legs crossed, his fingers propped together in front of his chest. When he looked up at her a little ripple of something passed through Caroline. Nerves, she decided. What else could it be?

"Graphology is the study of handwriting," she

said. "It's been researched primarily in Germany and France. That's where I learned the skill."

Stephen rose from his chair and began pacing, hands thrust deep in his trouser pockets, eyes studying the tips of his black shoes.

Caroline went on. "Handwriting is unique. Because there are so many different writing styles, it's unlikely that any two people would write precisely the same. By studying an individual's style, many things about the writer can be determined."

"Like what?" Richard asked.

"Personality traits, mostly," Caroline said. "Age can be determined to some degree. But no absolute distinguishing style can differentiate a man's and woman's handwriting. Sometimes samples indicate if a writer is left- or right-handed. It can't, however, tell things like nationality or race."

"Miss Sommerfield," Richard said, "at the party last week you mentioned that graphology is being used in Europe for criminal investigations."

Caroline nodded. "Yes, it's used for verification of signatures, for example, and in forgery cases."

Richard's smile broadened. "Come over here, Stephen. Let's see what she's come up with."

Stephen ventured closer, looking over Caroline's shoulder as she sorted through the handwriting samples Richard had given her. Heat from him caused her heart to thump a little faster.

She held up the first one. "This writer, I would say, is unimaginative, rather boring and preoccupied with money matters."

"Jenkins wrote this. He's Stephen's head accountant," Richard said. He turned to Stephen. "Dead accurate analysis, I'd say."

Caroline was pleased with herself, though Stephen only grunted noncommittally. She turned to the second sample.

"This person is a worrier," she said. "Indecisive, I'd imagine, and a little materialistic."

She glanced up at Richard, who smiled.

"Aunt Delfina," he said.

Stephen's eyebrows drew together, and Caroline guessed that analysis was correct as well, whoever Aunt Delfina was.

"The writer of this," she said, turning to the final sample, "is confident, enterprising and ambitious. But also obstinate, pigheaded and…sexually frustrated."

Stephen glared over her shoulder. "That's *my* handwriting."

He jerked the paper away from her and crumpled it up. Caroline saw crimson creep up from his shirt collar as her own cheeks warmed.

"Excellent demonstration, Miss Sommerfield," Richard said. "I think it's obvious that you have extraordinary talent in this field."

Stephen mumbled something and shoved the ball of paper into his pocket.

"Excuse me, sir." Charles spoke from the doorway. "Your carriage is at your disposal."

A little pang of disappointment thumped in Caroline's stomach. She hadn't wanted to be here, had been on edge since arriving, yet now was reluctant to go.

But it was for the best. She chanced another look at Stephen. He was again watching her. Yes, she decided, it was for the best that she leave.

She loaded her tools into her satchel.

"I'll walk you out," Richard said.

At the doorway, Caroline glanced at Stephen one last time. He stood staring out the dark window, his back to her.

"Happy birthday," she said.

He spun around, obviously surprised.

"Sorry you didn't get the gift you wanted." She glanced at the desk. "But the day's not over."

Stephen leaned forward slightly, then plopped into his chair.

How was he ever going to work in his office again?

Stephen stepped behind his desk and squared the ledgers and stacks of papers Richard had replaced while he was chasing down Caroline. But he didn't see the work that awaited him. He saw a naked woman. On his desk. His two favorite things in the whole world, together.

Stephen sank into his chair. Of course, the naked woman he imagined on his desk wasn't just any woman. It was Caroline Sommerfield.

He pulled loose his tie and popped open his collar. What a hell of a birthday.

"So, what do you think?" Richard asked, striding back into the office. "Isn't she wonderful? Isn't she everything I said she was?"

That and more. If only Richard knew.

Stephen leaned back in his chair. Richard was his assistant, and would have been a partner if he'd had the required financial backing. Still, he was indispensable. Stephen listened to him, trusted him, confided in him. And Richard had never let him down.

"I don't know…" Stephen said.

"You saw her evaluation of those handwriting samples," Richard said. "She had old Jenkins cold."

"That's true."

"And Delfina?" Richard grinned. "I like your dear, sweet aunt Delfi as much as anyone, but you have to admit that she is indecisive, just as Caroline said."

Stephen shrugged. He couldn't argue with Caroline's assessment of his aunt.

Richard chuckled. "She did a good job on you, too, Steve."

He sat forward, not the least amused by Caroline Sommerfield's determination of his own personality. Not that she wasn't accurate. He just didn't like being analyzed like a bug in a jar.

"Sexually frustrated." Richard laughed again. "Maybe I *should* have sent you a whore for your birthday."

"I can find my own women."

"Then why don't you?"

Stephen shifted in the chair. "I don't have time."

"Yes, you do," Richard said. "You have plenty of time. But you spend all of it working."

"I have a lot to do," Stephen grumbled.

"You don't have to prove anything to anyone," Richard said softly.

Stephen glanced up at him, then looked away.

"No one equates you with your father and what he did," Richard said.

Stephen dismissed his words with a wave of his hand. "Let's stick to business."

Richard just looked at him for a moment, then went on. "As I see it, Caroline can analyze the handwriting on Pickette's document and prove that it's fraudulent," he said. "The agreement he claims is genuine will be exposed as a hoax. Pickette will be gone, out of your hair, and should consider himself lucky if he doesn't end up in prison. Your problem will be solved."

"But can she prove that?"

"She's an expert in her field," Richard said. "She has letters of recommendation from Germany and France."

"Will anyone believe her here, in this country, in this city?" Stephen asked. "This graphology. Has anyone here even heard of it? Do they respect it? Believe in it?"

Richard shook his head. "No, not like in Europe."

"Then what good is it to me?"

Stephen pushed himself out of the chair and began pacing again. He rubbed his chin and stared at the floor. He did some of his best thinking like this.

He turned suddenly to Richard and snapped his fingers. "We could make her an expert."

"Make her one?" Richard asked. "How?"

"By giving her other work to do," Stephen said. "I've suspected for a while that someone on the warehouse crew is stealing. What if I put Caroline on the case? I'll get handwriting samples from all the employees and have her look for traits such as dishonesty, untrustworthiness."

Richard nodded slowly. "Yes, I see what you mean."

"We can't fire a man over a handwriting sample," Stephen said. "But we can determine the employees with those traits and have them watched. We just might turn up our thief."

"You could be onto something here," Richard said.

"I can use her to screen prospective job applicants. Weed out the questionable ones." Stephen gripped the back of his desk chair. "Once I've established her credibility here, I can loan her to other prominent businessmen in town."

Richard frowned. "That sounds like we're just using her."

"I'm giving her a chance to use this graphology thing she's so proud of," Stephen insisted. "Once the other businessmen see what she's capable of they can testify to her credentials. And when the Pickette case gets to court, Caroline will be the leading graphologist in Los Angeles and her word will be accepted."

"I don't know…"

"She wants to use this graphology skill of hers, doesn't she?"

"Yes," Richard said. "She applied with Pinkerton but they turned her down. She was very disappointed. She wanted that job. Her father sent her here from Europe to find a husband, but she wants to work instead.''

''Well, then, you see? I'm doing her a favor.''

''You're doing yourself a favor, Steve.''

Stephen's face hardened. ''I'm not going to let Russell Pickette make a fool out of me.''

A few moments of silence passed before Richard slapped his knee and rose from the chair. ''All right, we'll do it your way. And it just might work, as long...''

''As long as what?''

''As long as you're sure Pickette's document is really a forgery,'' Richard said.

Stephen started pacing again. Russell Pickette had been a pain in his side ever since he'd shown up two weeks ago waving a document that claimed he had title to a two-hundred-acre farm belonging to Stephen.

Stephen didn't know Russell Pickette personally. Had never met him. He recognized his name from the ledger book his accountant used to keep track of the semiannual rent Pickette paid on the acreage he farmed. It was a small amount. Insignificant, really.

Pickette didn't look like a con artist, or a thief, just a worn, weary farmer. But he was trying to defraud Stephen, just the same. Cheat him out of a prime piece of real estate, just when Stephen was about to pull together a large business deal involving that property.

Pacing behind his desk, Stephen got angry again

just thinking about Pickette. Then, as it always did, humiliation surged through him, deep in the pit of his stomach.

Pickette claimed the document had been written by Stephen's father, George Monterey. Stephen cringed at the memory.

George had died when Stephen was a boy, and Stephen still remembered what that felt like. Uncle Colin had agreed to take in him and his little brother, Thomas. Even now, standing in his office in the West Adams Boulevard home, Stephen remembered the day he and Thomas had arrived at Uncle Colin's home. Colin hadn't wanted them to forget, either. He'd had a photographer on hand that day to mark the occasion.

Still pacing, Stephen rubbed his hand over his chest. What his father had done still made him sick, all these years later.

He stopped, realizing Richard was speaking to him.

"What?" Stephen asked.

"I said, do you want to go ahead with this?" Richard asked.

Stephen was tired, but restless, too, for some reason. Memories of his father, that Pickette bastard, Uncle Colin—they filled his head tonight. But something else nagged at him, too. Something he couldn't pinpoint.

"Get her in here tomorrow," Stephen said. "Put her to work. I want to resolve this issue with Pickette."

"It might not be that simple," Richard said. "I don't think Caroline was all that happy to be here."

Stephen waved away his concern. "She'll take the job."

"All right. I'll talk with her first thing in the morning," Richard said, and headed for the door.

"Richard? I want you to keep this Pickette problem to yourself," Stephen said. "Miss Sommerfield doesn't need to know what I have planned for her just yet."

"I don't think that's a good idea," Richard said. "When she finds out, she's bound to think you set her up just so she'd testify on your behalf."

"I'll take care of Miss Sommerfield."

"Caroline Sommerfield looks like a handful," Richard said, grinning. "Are you sure you can handle her?"

Stephen sank into his desk chair. Of course he could handle her. But it would be a hell of a lot easier if he could stop thinking about her naked.

Chapter Four

"She said *no?*" Stephen rocked forward in his desk chair, glaring at Richard. "Caroline Sommerfield said no? She turned down my job offer?"

Richard nodded slowly and sank into the chair across from him. "Turned it down flat."

Morning sunlight beamed in through the open windows, brightening the room and bringing a little breeze with it.

"Did you explain to her that Monterey Enterprises is one of the largest, most prestigious corporations in the country?" Stephen demanded.

"I did."

"That I have holdings that reach around the world?"

"Yes," Richard said, "I told her that as well."

"That she should count herself damned lucky that I'm even considering her for a job?"

Richard rose. "I did that, Stephen. I told her all those things."

"Did you offer her the salary I specified?"

"Yes, and I even went beyond that figure," Richard said.

Stephen shoved away the reports he'd been looking at. "Then what the hell else does she want?"

Richard shrugged. "I don't know."

Stephen pushed himself out of his chair and started pacing. Until last night he'd never even heard of a graphologist. But now, this morning, he absolutely had to have one.

And not just because of those dreams he'd had last night.

Stephen mumbled a curse as he paced. Damn that Russell Pickette. That rogue wasn't going to get away with stealing his land, and he sure as hell wasn't going to make a fool of him.

Stephen stopped pacing. "I need that Sommerfield woman. And I don't care what it takes to get her here."

"I've tried everything."

"Then try something else."

"There is nothing else," Richard insisted.

Stephen pressed his lips together, fuming silently.

"I tried everything, Stephen. Her mind is firmly made up."

"We'll see about that...." Stephen grabbed his jacket and stalked out of the room.

When the bell jangled at the front door, Caroline bolted to her feet, nearly upsetting the teacups on her aunt's breakfast table.

"Caroline," Aunt Eleanor admonished, "let Bessie get the door. You know what's expected of servants."

Eleanor wasn't a wealthy woman, but moved in social circles that occasionally intersected the upper class. Her long-deceased husband had left her well off, with a nice home and a servant, both well past their prime. Bessie was maid, cook and personal secretary to Aunt Eleanor. The years were catching up to her.

But it wasn't Caroline's concern for Bessie's health that drove her from the breakfast table. It was her own aunt and the husband-hunting strategy session that was under way.

"Really, I don't mind," Caroline said, easing away from the table.

"If it's someone selling something, tell them we're not interested," Aunt Eleanor called.

Caroline beat a hasty retreat through the house. If a salesman were at the door, she'd beg him to come inside and she'd listen to his sales pitch all day, if she could. Anything to get away from Aunt Eleanor.

Already this morning Caroline had had a visitor. Richard Paxton. She'd thought she might run into him at a party sometime, since he moved in the same crowd as Aunt Eleanor, or perhaps encounter him at a luncheon or dinner party. Where she didn't expect to see him was on her doorstep bright and early in the morning.

And with a job offer. An offer of the job she'd dreamed of. But Caroline had told him no and sent him on his way without even letting him into the house.

Luckily, he'd come by before Aunt Eleanor had risen for the day, so Caroline hadn't had to make up a lie to explain his presence. She shuddered to think what her aunt might say if she knew what Caroline's real plans were. And surely she'd faint away if she ever found out where Caroline had been last night.

That whole unfortunate incident was best forgotten, Caroline decided, as she reached the front door. And that most definitely included Mr. Monterey.

Stephen.

The thought of him slowed her footsteps and tied a knot in her stomach. Her skin tingled, just as it had last evening in his office when he'd watched her every move and made it a little difficult for her to breathe.

Caroline shook her head, clearing her thoughts. That man was trouble. He did things to her—without even touching her. No, Stephen Monterey was better forgotten. She was glad to be rid of him, to have him out of her life. In fact, she hoped she never saw him again.

Caroline smoothed down the folds of her dress and opened the door.

Stephen stood on the porch.

She gasped, stared wide-eyed. Then slammed the door in his face.

What in the world was he doing here? Caroline

fell back against the door, pressing her hand to her forehead. Why on earth would he—

The doorbell rang again.

She ignored it.

It rang another time.

She ignored it again.

Once more, the bell rang.

Caroline whipped around and opened the door wide enough to squeeze her face into the crack.

"Would you just stop that?" she hissed.

The angles of his face drew into hard lines. "Miss Sommerfield—"

"Go away."

He squared his wide shoulders and glared at her, one eyebrow creeping upward. "Miss Sommerfield—"

"Shh!" Caroline glanced back through the house, praying her aunt wouldn't come to see what all the racket was about. She peeked out the door again.

"You have to leave," she said.

"I want to talk to you."

"We have nothing to discuss."

"We sure as hell do." He braced his arm against the door, forcing it open.

Caroline pushed back. "Don't come in here. I— I have a gun. I'll shoot you, I swear."

Stephen rolled his eyes. "Fire away."

She fell back into the foyer as he pushed his way inside. Darn, she was going to have to work on her lying. She couldn't fool one single soul.

Stephen closed the door, looking slightly annoyed. "This may come as a surprise to you, Miss Sommerfield, but there are literally dozens of people who would give their right arm to have me appear on their doorstep with an offer of employment."

"Keep your voice down." Caroline waved her hands at him and glanced over her shoulder again.

He craned his neck, following her line of vision. "Is something wrong?"

"No," she said quickly. "Of course not. Why would anything be wrong? Now look, Mr. Monterey, I appreciate your coming here, but I'm simply not interested. Good day. Please leave now."

He didn't budge.

She drew herself up taller, stretching her chin as high as it would go. "Mr. Monterey, I'm afraid I must insist that you—"

"Caroline? Caroline?"

She cringed. It was Aunt Eleanor, and by the sound of her voice she was drawing closer.

"Hurry." Caroline caught Stephen's arm and tugged him toward the door. He didn't budge. Didn't even sway. It was like pulling on a tree trunk.

"Mr. Monterey, you really must—"

"Why, Caroline, who have we here?"

She spun around as Aunt Eleanor glided into the foyer. Too late. She was trapped.

Caroline dropped Stephen's arm and stepped a discreet distance away.

"No one, Aunt Eleanor," she said. "Just some vagrant asking for a handout."

"Why, Caroline, how you do tease."

Aunt Eleanor crossed the room, her hand extended. She was a tall, thin woman with gray hair and an uninspired wardrobe. But she was the epitome of social graces, a gentlewoman who always did the right thing and never stopped striving for perfection. In others, as much as herself.

"I know quite well who this gentleman is," Aunt Eleanor said. "Mr. Monterey, it's so very nice to have you here. What a pleasant surprise. I'm Mrs. Eleanor Markham, Caroline's aunt."

Stephen removed his derby and took her hand. "Very nice to meet you, Mrs. Markham."

Her gaze shifted between the two of them. "I take it you've come to call on Caroline?"

His gaze settled on Caroline. "Actually, I have."

Aunt Eleanor fairly beamed with pleasure. A big smile stretched across her face and her eyes glazed over.

Caroline didn't blame her aunt. Stephen did look exceptionally handsome this morning. He wore a dark blue suit with pleated trousers and a high buttoned vest. His shirt, with its starched collar, was snowy white, contrasting with his gray-striped necktie.

But Stephen's good looks weren't what held Aunt Eleanor's attention. She'd spotted her prey—a highly eligible bachelor—and was plotting her next move.

"Caroline never mentioned that you two had met." Aunt Eleanor laughed gently. "And here I was planning another round of parties for her. Her father will be so pleased when he hears the news. And so quickly after arriving in the city, too.''

A slow smile spread over Stephen's face.

Caroline didn't like the look of that smile. Something was behind it. Something calculating. She cautioned herself to be on guard.

''Come into the parlor, Mr. Monterey,'' Aunt Eleanor said, guiding him to the room off the foyer. Stephen folded himself onto the peach settee and tucked his long legs behind a marble-topped table. Caroline considered making a break for the door while she still could, but didn't want to leave him at the mercy of her aunt; she didn't dislike him *that* much.

Aunt Eleanor took the chair directly across from Stephen. ''So, tell me, how did you two meet?'' she asked.

Caroline perched on the piano stool, the farthest seat from Stephen. Now was when better lying skills would come in handy. Her brain spun, trying to invent some reasonable story that didn't involve last night's escapade, when she'd been mistaken for a prostitute. Nothing came to her.

She sighed, forced to tell the truth. At least an abbreviated version of it.

''Actually, Aunt Eleanor, I was at Mr. Monterey's home last night,'' Caroline said. ''I stopped by to see a sick friend.''

Aunt Eleanor nodded. ''Oh, yes, your cousin Sophie said that you'd gone to visit someone on West Adams Boulevard.''

Caroline seethed. Darn her cousin. She'd promised not to tell. Goodness, relatives were proving to be more than inconvenient—a downright pain in the neck.

"So, who did you visit?" Aunt Eleanor asked.

Caroline pressed her lips together. "Well, actually—"

"My aunt," Stephen said.

A wave of profound gratitude washed over Caroline. Their gazes met and Stephen Monterey suddenly took on the look of a knight in the shiniest armor ever imagined.

"My aunt Delfina," Stephen explained. "Perhaps you know her, Mrs. Markham?"

"I've never had the pleasure, but I've heard of her, of course." Aunt Eleanor rose from her chair. "I'll have Bessie prepare us some tea. Caroline, do make Mr. Monterey comfortable."

Eleanor smiled knowingly and disappeared out of the parlor.

Caroline watched her leave, then turned to Stephen, and suddenly he didn't look like a knight in shining anything. He was smirking. Actually smirking. Oh, he was trying very hard to hide it, but that was definitely a smirk she saw on his face.

Caroline rose from the piano stool. "Why are you here?"

"I'm here about the position we discussed," he said.

The position on the desktop? Caroline bit into her

lip, forcing the image out of her head. Goodness, why couldn't she stop thinking about that?

"The position of graphologist," Stephen said.

"Oh, yes, of course."

"I'm here to convince you to accept my job offer," Stephen said.

"I don't want to work for you."

"*Everyone* wants to work for me."

He was pompous and arrogant...and devilishly good-looking. Caroline struggled to hold on to her anger against the onslaught of his masculine presence, which overwhelmed Aunt Eleanor's delicately furnished parlor. He was far too rugged for doilies and lace.

"I, Mr. Monterey, am not *everyone*." Caroline stared down at him, and it made her feel superior to do so.

That feeling lasted only a few more seconds, until Stephen rose from the settee and towered over her. He folded his arms across his chest.

"So, tell me, Miss Sommerfield, why do you refuse to come to work for me?"

There were a dozen reasons—and there were none. Caroline had lain awake most of the night reliving the short time she'd been in his house, in his presence. She'd tossed and turned, wrestling with emotions she'd never imagined before. Stephen had managed to take over most of her thoughts, somehow, and no one—not one single person—had ever done that.

He had consumed her, and the scary part was that

he would continue to do so. Caroline had sensed that in him the first moment they met, even though she couldn't put a name to the feeling at the time. He would devour her and all she believed in, until there was nothing left of herself.

Caroline eased away from him, needing the distance, hoping that space between them would ease the tension. It didn't.

"I don't need your job," she said.

His brow creased. "You didn't find work elsewhere?"

"No," she admitted. "But I realized that if Richard Paxton, then you, would recognize my skills and offer me employment, so would someone else. It's just a matter of time before another offer comes along."

Stephen's frown deepened. "Don't be so sure about that, Miss Sommerfield. I know every businessman in the city. If the wrong type of rumor got out about you…"

Stunned, she faced him again. "You'd—you'd do that? You'd ruin me?" she demanded.

"The business world can be very ugly, Miss Sommerfield."

"But that would be a lie! A bare-faced lie!"

Stephen glanced toward the parlor door. "Do you want your aunt back in here, asking questions?"

Caroline clamped her mouth shut, capping her anger but not stopping it.

"Won't your aunt be surprised to learn that your

real goal in coming to Los Angeles isn't to find a husband?'' he asked.

She felt violated. ''How did you know that?''

''Don't think I haven't seen that look in her eye before, on the face of countless other aunts, mothers and grandmothers,'' Stephen said. ''And tell me this, Miss Sommerfield, what would your aunt say if she found out your true desire is to work for the Pinkerton Detective Agency?''

Caroline's mouth flew open. ''Who told you?''

He pressed on. ''Would she be scandalized to learn that you want a job? I think she would be. In fact, she might even contact your father.''

Caroline's eyes narrowed. ''Why are you saying these things? Why are you doing this?'' She spun away and stalked to the window, struggling to hold her temper down. ''You're a wicked man,'' she said.

Yes, he was. Stephen knew that because at the moment he was having some very wicked thoughts.

He walked to the window and stood behind her, as close as he dared. Her hair was done up in a knot atop her head, with a few tendrils curling loose. He wanted to lean his head down and press his mouth against that lovely neck of hers. Ease himself closer until her soft body cushioned his. Loop his arms around her and cup her breasts in his palms.

Oh, yes, he was a very wicked man.

Caroline shifted, keeping her chin high and her shoulders straight. The movement rustled her clothing, and Stephen imagined peeling away all those layers. Lace, silk, bows, ribbons, all waiting there for him to discover...and discard.

"I'm glad I slapped you last night," Caroline said, still refusing to turn away from the window.

He deserved that slap. And he could probably use another right now. Something to bring him back to reality and restore a little sanity to his thoughts. He'd been almost continuously aroused since he'd laid eyes on her last night, and he never did his best thinking in that state. In fact, he could hardly think at all. Except about one thing.

On the way over here this morning he'd planned what he'd say to her. Richard had told him how she wanted to work for Pinkerton, and that she'd been sent to Los Angeles to find a husband. He'd intended to use that against her, threaten to tell her aunt, force Caroline to come to work for him.

Running an international corporation meant using what means were at his disposal to get what he wanted. Tough problems needed tough solutions sometimes. And that was all right with Stephen. He liked getting his way.

But this time, with Caroline, it brought him no pleasure. No business opponent had ever looked hurt before, as Caroline did. None had made him feel ashamed, as she had.

She turned then, her chin still high. Her nearness hummed through Stephen. She smelled rich and earthy. If he moved forward, just the tiniest bit, he could touch her.

Instead he forced himself to back up a step.

"It appears you've left me no choice," she said.

She held herself rigid, clinging to her dignity and pride despite the fact he'd forced her to do it his way. The desire to kiss her roiled through Stephen. He wanted to replace that hurt look with pleasure, make her smile again.

But the image of Russell Pickette appeared in Stephen's mind, along with the memory of his father. He wouldn't let either of them get the best of him. For that he needed Caroline. And now he had her.

"All right, Mr. Monterey, I'll accept your job," she said. "But this is strictly business. No personal involvement of any kind."

Stephen nodded. "Of course. I wouldn't have it any other way."

Chapter Five

Aunt Eleanor glided into the parlor, still smiling.

"Bessie will have tea for us in a moment," she said.

Stephen retrieved his derby from the table. "That's very kind of you, Mrs. Markham, but Caroline and I are going out."

"You are?" she asked.

"We are?" Caroline echoed.

Stephen turned to her. "We are."

"But—"

"You should bring a wrap," Stephen said. "We'll likely be out until late."

"But… Now?"

Stephen smiled. "No sense in waiting."

Caroline planted her hands on her hips. "Did it occur to you, Mr. Monterey, that I might already have plans for today?"

He shrugged indifferently. "No, not for a minute."

"Run along, Caroline, dear," Aunt Eleanor said. "You mustn't keep Mr. Monterey waiting."

Caroline threw Stephen a sour look and left the room in a huff.

Aunt Eleanor waved goodbye from the front porch a few minutes later as Caroline rode away in Stephen's carriage, with him seated across from her.

"Well, I hope you're happy," Caroline said, and jerked her chin at him.

He nodded. "I'm very happy."

"Do you always get your way?"

"Most always."

"Then I suggest you brace yourself for a few disappointments, Mr. Monterey," Caroline told him. "You'll find that I'm not like everyone else you know."

He smiled a slow, lazy smile. "I'm already aware of that, Miss Sommerfield."

Caroline tugged on her skirt and turned her face to the window, ignoring him.

Since she refused to speak to him, Caroline had to content herself with watching the homes of the West Adams district roll past the carriage window. In the morning sunlight, with their large green lawns, swaying palms and ferns, stone walls and wrought-iron fences, they were even more impressive than when she'd seen them last night.

The homes displayed a variety of grand architecture. There were storybook houses with gingerbread and scrollwork, great stone castles, English Tudors, white brick Colonials with Grecian columns.

The carriage swung into the driveway of Stephen's home. The brownstone looked bigger, more imposing that it had last night. Witches' caps topped the circular turrets on the house's four corners. Balconies opened on the second story. Massive stone chimneys and dormers punctuated the steep roof.

"My uncle Colin and I designed the house," Stephen said, gesturing out the window. "It's on two acres, one of the biggest lots in the city."

"It is a beautiful home," she agreed.

"Seven bedrooms, not including the servants' quarters. A trophy room, a card room, a billiard room, several sitting rooms and parlors, a formal dining room and breakfast room, and probably several other rooms I've never been in." He smiled. "We had marble brought in from Italy. The stained glass windows are from France. Aunt Delfi always has some decorating project going on."

The carriage stopped. Stephen climbed out and helped her down. Richard waited on the front steps. He broke into a full smile when Caroline stepped out of the carriage.

"Miss Sommerfield is starting work today, Richard," Stephen announced, and presented her as if she were a trophy from a big game hunt.

"Welcome, Miss Sommerfield," he said. "I'm glad you changed your mind."

"Thank you," Caroline said. She liked Richard and wouldn't be rude to him, even though she might have decidedly different feelings for Stephen.

The front door opened and the butler stepped outside.

"Excuse me, Mr. Monterey. Your aunt asks that you come to her at once."

Stephen nodded, then excused himself and went inside. Richard stepped over to Caroline.

"His aunt Delfina," he explained. "The slightly materialistic, indecisive worrier."

Caroline remembered her from the handwriting sample last night. "Oh, yes. Her. Is she ill?"

"Aunt Delfina?" Richard chuckled. "She's never had a genuine illness in her life. But that doesn't stop her from being a…situation that Stephen must contend with. He has several…situations."

Caroline was certain she'd been one of those situations this morning. What did that make her now? No longer a situation, had she been clicked over into the "dealt with" category?

"Well, I suppose we'd better go in," Richard said.

But instead he stood there gazing toward the far corner of the house for so long that Caroline turned and looked also.

"Is something wrong?" she asked.

"What?" He turned back. "Oh, no. I just…I just wanted to mention that you should see the grounds. They're impressive."

Caroline wasn't all that anxious to go inside, so if Richard wanted to stand here casting glances toward the corner of the house, that was fine with her.

"Should I see them now?" she asked.

"See what?"

"The grounds."

Richard shook his head, as if clearing his

thoughts. "No, no, we'd better get inside. Stephen will be…" His gaze drifted away again, but after a few seconds he caught himself. "Well," he said briskly. "Let's get inside before—"

Shouts came from the corner of the house, turning them both in that direction. A moment later a little boy rounded the corner, running toward them at full steam, short legs churning, arms pumping.

"Uncle Richard!"

A smile broke over Richard's face as he walked toward the child, scooped him up and swung him in a big circle. The boy squealed as Richard lifted him high overhead, then settled him into his arms.

Caroline couldn't help but be drawn to the two of them, laughing together, both so thoroughly happy to see one another.

"And who do we have here?" Caroline asked.

Richard turned so that she could see the child in his arms. Her breath caught. Black hair. Huge green eyes. Good gracious, the boy looked exactly like Stephen.

It hadn't occurred to her that he might be married. Or have a child. A huge weight settled on her chest.

"This is Joseph Thomas Monterey." Richard tickled the boy's chin. "Say hello to Miss Caroline, Joey."

The boy giggled and turned his attention away from Richard long enough to hold up four chubby fingers.

"I'm this many," he declared.

"Four years old?" Caroline nodded in pretended

surprise. "Goodness, you're an old man now, aren't you?"

Joey giggled again and threw his arms around Richard's neck. "Play, Uncle Richard, come play with me!"

"You're his uncle?" Caroline asked.

"Honorary title," Richard said, struggling to hold the squirming boy in his arms.

"And so Mr. Monterey would be his..."

"Uncle," Richard said. "Stephen is his uncle."

"Oh..."

"You gots to play with me, Uncle Richard." Joey tugged on his neck. "You gots to. Miss Brenna is too slow."

Richard's eyebrows rose in exaggerated surprise. "Is she?"

"Yes," Joey insisted. "She can't catch a ball, or nothing."

Richard gazed toward the corner of the house. "And where is Miss Brenna this morning?"

A moment later a young woman sprinted around the corner, holding up her skirt. When she saw them she froze for an instant, then walked over, hurriedly smoothing down wisps of her dark hair.

She stopped a few feet away. "Good morning, Mr. Paxton."

Despite the child in his arms, Richard straightened his tie. "Good morning, Miss Winslow."

The two of them looked at each other, then looked away.

"Good morning," Caroline said, and introduced herself.

"I'm very pleased to meet you," she said. "I'm Brenna Winslow, Joey's nanny."

Brenna was about her own age, Caroline guessed. Slender, with dark hair and deep brown eyes. Pretty. Richard seemed to think so, too.

"I'm starting work here today," Caroline said.

"What type of employment?"

"I'm working in Mr. Monterey's office," Caroline said, not wanting to explain yet again what a graphologist was.

"Welcome," Brenna said. She turned to Joey. "Come along, sweetie."

"I'll come out and play with you in a while," Richard promised, as he set Joey on the ground.

The boy looked up at him with his big green eyes. "Promise?"

Richard winked. "You bet."

Joey took Brenna's hand and skipped across the yard, pulling her along with him. She glanced back and waved.

Richard waved, and his hand froze in the air for a few seconds.

"He's adorable," Caroline said.

"Who?" Richard gave himself a little shake. "Joey, you mean. Yes, he's something, all right. Rough life, though, for such a little fellow. His mother…abandoned him."

"Oh, dear."

"Joey lives here," Richard said, still watching them cross the yard. "Brenna…Brenna takes good care of him."

Even after the two of them disappeared around

the house, Richard stood there for a few minutes, then finally gestured toward the stone steps leading inside.

"We'd better go," he said. "Stephen is waiting."

And so was her new life. Caroline drew in a big breath and headed up the steps.

As Charles greeted them, Caroline glanced at the sitting room off to her left, the place where she'd first seen Stephen. Last night seemed like a year ago.

There were many things she hadn't noticed about the house yesterday evening—the red marble entry, the intricately carved ash woodwork, the ceilings painted with elaborate scenes. Stephen was rightfully proud of his home.

When Caroline and Richard arrived at Stephen's office, Caroline's heart thumped its way into her throat. Last night. The desk. His offer to undress her.

Caroline silently admonished herself for having such thoughts. Regardless of the circumstances, here she was, one of the pioneer women in the workplace. And all she could think of was Stephen Monterey's desire to make love to her in her hat and high buttoned shoes. Disgraceful!

Caroline pulled herself up to stand a little straighter.

True, she didn't know exactly how an employee should act. She'd never known a woman who actually had a job. But men did it. How difficult could it be?

One thing was certain. Thoughts of her employer—at least *those* kinds of thoughts—should be put out of her head.

She followed Richard into the office. Stephen wasn't there.

"He might need rescuing from his aunt. I'll be right back. Make yourself comfortable," Richard said, and left her alone.

Comfortable? A ridiculous notion.

Caroline wandered through the big room, situated at the corner of the house. A row of windows ran down one side of the office, around the circular turret and across the back. Paintings of animals and hunting scenes hung on the walls. The furniture consisted of heavy walnut pieces that looked very masculine.

She caught a glimpse of herself in the beveled mirror above the stone fireplace and straightened her hat. When she'd dressed this morning she'd had no idea she'd end up with a job before noon, but was glad she'd worn a take-me-seriously dark green shirtwaist.

Caroline studied her reflection for a few minutes. She was taking the first step down a path she'd be hard-pressed to return from. Accepting a job. Working. Not many thought it proper.

Aunt Eleanor would not be pleased. In fact, she'd be horrified when she found out. Caroline wasn't quite sure how she'd explain this to her.

The notion of women in the workplace was accepted in progressive circles—circles that were very tiny. Hopefully, by the time she returned home this evening she could come up with some plausible excuse for her absence. And what she'd do about tomorrow and the day after, Caroline had no idea.

She didn't even want to think about how Aunt Eleanor would react when she found out Stephen Monterey wasn't courting her.

Despite the fact that she hadn't wanted this particular job—really, this particular boss—working was the only thing that made sense to Caroline. The alternative was marriage. She cringed at the thought of being stuck in the same house, mindlessly preparing menus, overseeing the mundane activities of a household, never going anyplace new, seeing anything different.

She couldn't imagine why her father thought she'd like such a life. Since her mother's death when she was ten years old, the two of them had traveled Europe, living in hotels or as guests in fine homes, never staying in the same location for more than a few weeks or months. Always new places to see, new people to meet. How could anyone find contentment with the same man, one house—forever?

Caroline adjusted her hat again and gave herself a nod of encouragement in the mirror. Even though she'd been coerced into accepting this position, she was glad she had it. Because after today, she might not have to worry about a ghastly future of *marriage* ever again.

And to think she had Stephen Monterey to thank for that.

Chapter Six

Caroline roamed the office, waiting. She strolled past the windows overlooking the rear of the house. As Richard had said, the grounds were magnificent. Brick walkways wound among palms and ferns and beds of blooming flowers. Water in a large fountain bubbled up, then cascaded down its three tiers.

Under a shady, fruitless mulberry, Joey played. Brenna managed to keep up with him. Caroline saw them both laughing, and that made her smile.

She wandered through the office again and stopped at a glass curio cabinet filled with delicate china figurines. Caroline opened the door for a closer look. There was a prancing horse, an old man with a fishing pole, a mother cradling a baby to her breast, a tiger, a clown. Of the two dozen or so in the collection, each was beautifully sculpted in intricate detail.

On the other side of the cabinet were music boxes. Some were made of rich woods, others encrusted with gems, all fashioned in a variety of shapes. There were simple boxes, elaborate musical instruments, treasure chests.

The collection was stunning. Their music must be lovely, as well. Caroline reached inside to open the lid on a tiny rosewood piano.

"Don't touch that."

Startled, she spun around. Stephen glared at her from the doorway. She felt like a child with her hand caught in the cookie jar.

"I—I just wanted to hear the music," Caroline said.

He crossed the room, with the force of his presence causing her to move away.

"Is this your collection?" she asked, staring up at his big, wide back.

"Yes, and don't touch them." Stephen closed the cabinet door firmly. "Please."

"They're beautiful," she said. "Don't you want to hear the music?"

"They're here to look at, not touch," Stephen said.

A cabinet full of music boxes that weren't allowed to be played? That was certainly odd, but Caroline let it go.

Stephen pulled a white handkerchief from his pocket and briskly wiped away the fingerprints left on the cabinet's glass door.

"I'm sorry," Caroline said. "I didn't know your collection was not to be touched."

"Well, now you know."

"Indeed I do," she said.

Stephen stuffed his handkerchief into his pocket. "Let's get down to business."

He seemed to be trying hard to maintain distance from her, or perhaps this was just how an employer should behave, Caroline thought as she followed him to his desk. Either way, she was grateful, because ever since she'd entered this house she'd been on edge. Should having a job make one feel this way? she wondered.

"Please, sit down, Miss Sommerfield." He indicated the chair in front of his desk.

Caroline perched on the edge of the seat and smoothed her skirt. She gazed up at him expectantly.

He looked at her hat—the crown, with its array of bows and flowers, then the brim, which framed her face. Suddenly, Stephen plopped into his chair and pulled his gaze away.

"First of all..." He tugged at his collar and cleared his throat. "First of all, Miss Sommerfield, let me welcome you to my company. I realize we got off to somewhat of a rocky start—"

"Somewhat, to say the least," Caroline said.

Stephen cleared his throat again. "I have a few requirements of my employees. I expect loyalty. I expect you to be trusting in any assignment you are given. I don't expect to be questioned concerning my intentions or motives. Is that clear?"

"Maybe you should just buy a dog."

He blinked across the desk at her. "I beg your pardon?"

"I will not be blindly loyal or obedient, Mr. Monterey," she told him. "If that's what you expect, you will be sadly disappointed."

Stephen seemed lost for a moment. Apparently, this was his new-employee speech and no one had ever challenged him on it before. Probably because everyone else had been desperate to work for him, and Caroline wasn't.

Stephen shifted in the chair, mentally trying to find his place again. "Yes, well, as I was saying, Miss Sommerfield, as an employee of Monterey Enterprises you'll be expected to arrive on time for work each day. And you will remain here the entire day, unless given permission to leave early."

"Here again, Mr. Monterey, you will find a trained animal suits your needs better," Caroline said. "A collie or perhaps a shepherd. Something you can keep locked up until needed, then trotted out to perform on demand."

"Miss Sommerfield—" Stephen forced himself to pull in a calming breath and gave her a stiff smile. "Miss Sommerfield, I assure you that these things aren't—"

"Good, I see you two are already getting things handled." Richard came into the office carrying a stack of papers.

"I was just explaining to Miss Sommerfield that she will share the office with Mr. Turley." Stephen rolled his eyes toward Caroline. "Unless you'd prefer I build you a kennel out back."

"Come along, Caroline," Richard said. "I'll get you settled and show you around a bit."

But before she could rise from the chair, another woman bustled into the office. She was portly, with carefully coiffed gray hair. A frown creased her forehead.

"Stephen, dear. Oh, Stephen. Everything is in a *complete* uproar."

"We just settled everything a few minutes ago, Aunt Delfi," Stephen said as he rose from his chair. "We have a complete uproar now?"

"Something *must* be done," Delfi declared, and dropped a book of fabric samples on his desk. "The decorator. He's *insisting* that I give him my decision. *Insisting,* Stephen, *insisting.* And the menus. The menus haven't been planned. Cook is ready to walk off. *Walk off,* I tell you. And as if that weren't enough, the gardeners want to know about the azaleas. *Azaleas,* Stephen."

He guided her to the chair beside Caroline and seated her. "Aunt Delfi, these are a few situations you need to handle this morning, but—"

"An *uproar,*" she insisted. "And where *were* you last night? During the *party?* You disappeared. Where did you go? Did something come up?"

Stephen dropped into his chair again. He glanced at Caroline. "Yes, Aunt Delfi, something did… come up."

Richard coughed and moved away to the windows in the corner.

"But *what?*" Delfi demanded. "You left your

own party. Was it something urgent? Something big?"

Stephen shuffled papers across his desk. "Actually, yes, it was very big."

Delfina moaned. "But your own *party,* Stephen. People were *talking.* You know what I've been through since your uncle died. You know how difficult it is to maintain proper appearances. How could you have *done* such a thing?"

Stephen gestured to Caroline. "Aunt Delfi, I'd like you to meet Caroline Sommerfield. Miss Sommerfield, my aunt, Delfina Monterey."

Delfina grabbed Caroline's hand. "You *do* understand what I'm saying, don't you, dear?"

"Of course," Caroline said. Appearances were everything, especially among the upper class.

"Of course," Delfina echoed. She turned back to Stephen and wagged her fingers at the fabric samples. "Now, what are we going to *do?*"

"I'll take care of the decorator, Aunt Delfi," he promised.

"And the menus?" Delfina waved a leather-bound notebook in the air. "Should we have duck? Chicken? We always have chicken on Sundays, but lately…"

Stephen reached across the desk and relieved her of the notebook. "I'll handle the menus."

She pressed her hand to her bosom. "Oh, thank you, Stephen. You're such a dear. Now, the azaleas. The gardener is—"

"I'll speak with the gardener, too."

"Well…" Delfina drew in a cleansing breath. "It makes one feel so good to have accomplished something."

Stephen smiled faintly at his aunt. "I'll have everything handled as soon as Miss Sommerfield is settled."

"Settled?" Delfina asked. "Settled where?"

"Miss Sommerfield will be working for me," Stephen said.

Delfina turned to Caroline and looked her up and down. Worry lines crept into her forehead again. "In what capacity?"

"She'll be working here in the office," Stephen explained.

"*Working?* In your *office?*" Delfina's eyes widened and her mouth tightened to a horrified pucker. "A *woman?* Working? In our home? What will people *say?*"

"Aunt Delfi," Stephen said, "it's nothing to get upset over."

"Nothing to get *upset* over?" Delfina turned to Caroline. "You must not take this personally, my dear. I'm sure you're quite good at whatever it is you do. But Stephen, you can't do this. You simply *can't.*"

"It's done, Aunt Delfi," Stephen said. "Miss Sommerfield is—"

"People are *already* talking. What will they say when they find out? A young woman coming and going from our home every day. *Working* here," Delfina wailed. *"Working!"*

Stephen circled the desk and knelt beside her. He patted her arm. "Aunt Delfi, there's no other way around this. I need Miss Sommerfield and—"

Caroline shot to her feet. "I'll just leave."

"No, you won't." Stephen rose from beside his aunt's chair. "You're not going anywhere."

"But your aunt is terribly upset," Caroline said. "I simply couldn't live with myself knowing how I'd upset her."

Stephen pointed his finger at her. "I know what you're trying to do, and—"

"My *hands!*" Delfina thrust her hands out in front of her. "I've lost the feeling in both my little fingers!"

Stephen looked down at his aunt. "Your little fingers are fine, Aunt Delfi—"

"My *thumbs!* They're going, too!"

"Aunt Delfi," Stephen said patiently, "Miss Sommerfield is here for a very important matter."

"It's not really all that important," Caroline said.

He glared at her. "Aunt Delfi, listen to me. Lots of women are working these days."

"But—" Delfina stopped suddenly and shifted her gaze from one side of the room to the other. "Does anyone else hear that bell ringing?"

Stephen groaned softly. "There's no bell ringing. Look, Aunt Delfi, you're going to have to—"

"It's getting louder." Delfina's gaze roamed the room. "Louder, I tell you."

"Aunt Delfi..." Stephen pulled at his collar.

"Caroline could always move in," Richard said.

Everyone turned to him, staring, then swung around to Caroline. She felt her cheeks turn pink.

Stephen found his voice first. "She could... what?"

Richard shrugged. "Caroline could move in. As a guest of Delfina, of course."

Delfina's eyes narrowed and she cast a glance at Caroline. "My houseguest?"

"Of course," Richard said. "Caroline's family is well-known in Europe. Her father is very well respected there."

"He is?" Delfina and Stephen asked together.

They both stared, causing Caroline's cheeks to turn a shade redder.

"Mr. Sommerfield is a renowned criminologist, actually," Richard said. "He's sought after all over the Continent by the wealthy, the aristocracy, even the royals."

"Royalty?" Delfina asked, smiling now. "Really? Royalty? Oh, how *delightful*."

"Caroline would make a perfect houseguest," Richard said. "Under that guise, she could work here for such time as her services are needed. Don't you think so, Stephen?"

He looked at Caroline, his mouth open. She stared back, eyes wide.

"Well, I think it's a positively *wonderful* idea!" Delfina declared.

"So, Caroline," Richard asked, "how about it?"

Caroline simply stood there, letting it all sink in. She would be a houseguest? Here?

While it was true that she and her father had moved among the aristocracy in Europe, they were by no means wealthy people. But she was accustomed to that life and knew how to live it. She and her father had been among the entourage of some of Europe's finest families.

All this had started because she wanted to practice her profession, have a job where she could employ her skills, gain enough experience so that she could present herself to the Pinkerton Detective Agency with some degree of credibility.

She simply wanted to avoid getting married.

And somehow she'd ended up with a job she didn't ask for, a boss she didn't want—living here with Aunt Delfina? And *Stephen?*

"Well, Caroline?" Richard asked.

"Oh, you must," Delfina said. "You simply *must.*"

"It seems the best solution," Richard said. "Don't you think?"

"Well, I don't know…"

She turned to Stephen and saw he was as uncomfortable as she. A deep current flowed between them. She shouldn't stay. She knew it. He knew it.

He looked so troubled, so distressed that Caroline forgot her own discomfort with the situation. She wanted to smooth away the creases in his forehead. Brush her fingertips against the tight line of his lips. Rub his shoulders until they relaxed.

For an instant Caroline thought Stephen could see into her thoughts, into her soul. That somehow he knew she was thinking about him. Her heart pounded harder with this sudden, unexpected connection to him.

But Stephen looked away quickly, breaking the fragile link between them.

"I don't mean to push you, Caroline," Richard said, "but we need your answer."

If she said no, would Stephen make good on his threat? Would she be back to analyzing handwriting at parties? How much longer would it be before Aunt Eleanor completely forbade her to do it again?

And the worst prospect, Caroline thought, was that her aunt might really come up with a husband for her. Gracious, what would she do then?

Stephen pushed his hand through his hair and shrugged his wide shoulders. "If you stay here, you won't need to concern yourself with your aunt," he pointed out.

That was true. At least here, in the Monterey home, she'd be safe from Aunt Eleanor's matchmaking schemes. In fact, her aunt would be pleased that she was a guest in one of the most respected homes in Los Angeles. If this wasn't fertile husband-hunting ground, what was?

Caroline sighed resolutely. "All right. I'll stay."

"Excellent. I'm so *pleased*. Really, I'm so pleased." Delfina rose from her chair and her smile disappeared. "Oh, dear. I have to prepare your room. In fact, I have a dozen things to do now. Oh dear, oh *dear*."

Delfina left the room mumbling.

"Another crisis diverted." Richard followed Delfina out of the office, smiling and humming to himself.

The big office closed in around Caroline. Stephen seemed taller, wider. The distance between them shrank.

"So, you've gotten your way again," Caroline said.

"This wasn't my idea."

"But you didn't try to discourage your aunt," Caroline said. "I'm here to do a job. Nothing more. I suggest you remember that."

Stephen watched the sway of her skirt as she marched out of the room. How could he forget?

Chapter Seven

Packing, moving out of her aunt's house should have brought sadness to Caroline. After all, she'd lived there for a month now. It had become her home. And Aunt Eleanor was family.

Instead, Caroline tossed her belongings into her trunks and was away from the house with a peck on her aunt's cheek, a wave from the carriage and not even a backward look.

Further proof, Caroline decided as she headed toward West Adams Boulevard, that she wasn't meant to be married.

Living in one place made her restless, so leaving her aunt's house had been easy, almost welcome. She'd formed no bond with her aunt, her blood kin, so parting had been a breeze. Consequently, if she couldn't live in one place and couldn't stick with one person, how would she possibly be satisfied with married life?

She couldn't. And that was all right with Caroline.

Charles took charge of her trunks when she arrived, and Delfina took charge of her.

"It was so generous of your family to allow you to be our guest," Delfina said. "I'm sure they hated to see you go."

Actually, Aunt Eleanor had almost pushed her out the door. Being a houseguest of the Monterey family was nothing to be taken lightly. Once Aunt Eleanor spread the word among her friends, she'd surely be the envy of her circle.

"My aunt Eleanor," Caroline said, "was pleased that you invited me."

"Do you think your aunt would like to come to tea sometime?"

She'd probably stampede right over Charles, if invited.

Caroline smiled. "It's very gracious of you to ask."

"Well, we must get acquainted," Delfina insisted, hooking her arm in hers and leading her through the house.

Caroline glanced toward the suite of offices where she was supposed to be working. "But I think Mr. Monterey is expecting me."

"Stephen is *working*. He's always working," Delfina said. "We must have tea first."

Delfina guided her to the doorway of a sitting room decorated in deep green and oak.

"Isn't this a lovely room?" she asked.

The view from the French doors gave the room

its charm, opening onto the rose garden on the west side of the house.

"Yes," Caroline said. "It's very nice."

"I hate it...I think."

"But you just said—"

Delfina shivered. "Too dark. *Depressing.* I want it redone in something light, I believe. A lady's room. But that *decorator.* Oh, dear, that decorator. *Pushing* me all the time for decisions. Well, I'm sure Stephen will come up with a perfectly lovely color scheme."

"Mr. Monterey is picking out the decor of a lady's sitting room?"

"Oh, yes. Stephen takes care of *everything,*" Delfina said. Her lips drew together in concentration. "That reminds me. I must speak with Stephen about the spring cleaning. It should be *under way* already, but the schedule hasn't been passed along to the staff yet."

"Mr. Monterey runs the household staff as well?" Caroline asked.

"Of course. His uncle Colin took care of all these things, and since he passed away last winter Stephen has stepped in, naturally," Delfina said.

"But didn't Stephen run the business while his uncle oversaw everything else?" Caroline asked.

"Oh, yes," Delfina said. "Now Stephen does *both.*"

No wonder he had those little worry lines around his eyes, Caroline realized.

"If you'd like," she said, "I could help you organize the staff for the cleaning."

Delfina blinked up at her. "*Me?* Organize the staff?"

"Actually, I meant that I could assist you."

"Really?" Delfina's eyebrows crept together. "You could do that? Organize the staff?"

It was simply a matter of deciding what needed cleaning, insuring staff and supplies were in place, making assignments and then supervising. Not a big task at all.

"I'm certain," Caroline said.

Delfina frowned. "I don't know. That seems like a great *many* decisions to me."

"Nothing I can't handle," Caroline said. She smiled. "And in the process, you could give me a tour of this beautiful home."

Delfina pursed her lips. "Well, all right. I suppose we could *try*. I'll ask Stephen if he—"

"I don't think you should do that," Caroline said.

"Why?"

Because she was here to work as a graphologist, not organize the spring cleaning. Caroline doubted Stephen would be too keen on her jumping into that project, taking time away from the task she was being paid for.

But organizing the staff was such a simple matter. She'd seen Stephen's desk piled high with reports, correspondence, ledgers. He certainly had more important matters to attend to. Caroline didn't mind helping out...helping Stephen.

"We'll tell him when we're done," Caroline said. "I think he'll be very pleased that you handled the cleaning yourself."

Delfina thought for a moment, then finally nodded. "Well, all right."

"Do you have something we could make notes on?"

"Notes?" Delfina sighed heavily. "Now, you see, things are getting *complicated.*"

"If you'll just point me toward a tablet," Caroline said quickly, "I'll handle the note taking."

"Well, all right, then. There's one in the sitting room down the hallway. I'll fetch it."

Delfina trundled out the door, and Caroline couldn't help but wonder what she'd gotten herself into.

Stephen squared the thick stack of papers in front of him and started over again on the top line. He'd expected this report from his man in Johannesburg three weeks ago and was anxious to find out what was going on over there.

But he couldn't get through the first page. In fact, he couldn't get past the first paragraph.

Stephen determinedly focused his eyes on the words, only to find his mind drifting away again. He stopped and drummed his fingers on the desk. How was he supposed to concentrate when his new employee was being deliberately disobedient?

He glanced at the clock above the mantel. Caroline had returned twenty-one minutes ago. He knew because he'd pressed his face against the window-pane and watched the carriage pull up, seen her alight, seen the afternoon sun glow against her cheeks. He'd heard her voice in the vestibule, floating toward him like the music of last night's orchestra.

He slumped against his desk, remembering....

The words of the report in front of him came into sharp focus, reminding him that he had a business to run.

But Stephen pushed the report away. He had a more immediate problem to deal with. Obviously Caroline needed additional instruction on what was expected of his employees. She should have reported to his office promptly. It seemed he needed to explain a few things to her.

Better to handle these problems when they occurred. Stephen rose, tugged on his vest and strode out of his office.

Finding her was not a problem. He didn't need to ask Charles, call out her name, hunt through every room. Stephen only had to sniff the air. That scent...Caroline's scent. His nose guided him to the sitting room off the rose garden.

He stopped at the doorway. A pain tightened his chest at the sight of Caroline strolling through the room, her hands clasped in front of her. Graceful fingers...

Her lips were pressed together as she studied the painting above the marble fireplace. Full, pink lips...

Tiny lines of concentration wrinkled her forehead and rounded her big, expressive eyes.

She drew in a deep breath, which lifted her breasts higher, tighter against her blouse.

The pain in Stephen's chest arrowed downward with predictable results. He braced his arm against the wall and rested his head on his forearm.

How could this keep happening to him? Every time he looked at Caroline Sommerfield his body reacted this way. He had to get control of himself. He couldn't—

"Mr. Monterey?"

He jumped. Caroline peered out the doorway, her big blue eyes looking up at him.

"Are you all right?" she asked.

"Of course." Stephen tugged on his vest. "Of course I'm all right."

"I heard you groan," she said.

"I didn't groan," he insisted.

"Actually, it was more of a moan."

Stephen gritted his teeth. Well, all right, he might have moaned, but he certainly couldn't admit to it.

He straightened his shoulders. Better to get his mind on business, quickly.

"Miss Sommerfield, there is something we need to discuss."

"Certainly." She gazed up at him, her eyes bright.

Good heavens, what had he wanted to tell her? Stephen pulled on his necktie, trying to remember. It was something important, he was sure of that.

Dammit, he just couldn't think straight in this condition.

"Yes, Mr. Monterey?" she prompted.

"Well, Miss Sommerfield...I..."

She was so damned pretty. That thought pulsed in his mind, in his body. Even though he'd seen countless pretty women before, there was something different about Caroline. He couldn't say what it was. But it made his chest hurt, his stomach ache and the rest of him—

"Your aunt is serving tea," Caroline said. "Are you joining us?"

"Tea?" Stephen shook his head, finally remembering why he'd come looking for Caroline. "No, no tea. We're supposed to be working."

She grinned. "And I thought you served tea to welcome all your new employees. That's not true?"

Stephen smiled. He couldn't help it. "Just the newly hired graphologists."

She dipped her lashes. "I wasn't expecting this special attention."

"But you deserve it." The words slipped out in a whispered rush. He hadn't meant to say them.

Caroline lifted her head and her gaze met his. He could stay lost forever in her eyes.

She turned away and pointed to the mantel inside the sitting room.

"I was looking at the photographs," she said. "Your family?"

Glad for something else to concentrate on, Stephen followed her inside.

"My uncle Colin commissioned a photographer to take the family photographs a year or so ago." He pointed to the silver-framed photo on the right edge of the mantel. "This is my uncle."

Caroline studied the man. Older, with a full head of hair, he stood straight and tall—a man used to being in charge of his world. She saw the resemblance to Stephen.

"Your aunt takes a nice picture," Caroline said, of the next photograph.

Stephen smiled. "It took us three days to narrow down which gown she'd wear, but yes, she does look nice."

They moved to the next photograph. "And this is you, of course."

The camera's lens had captured Stephen's good looks, though he seemed to be trying to camouflage them with a somber expression.

Stephen pointed to the next photograph. "This is my nephew."

"Joey. I met him this morning with his nanny."

Caroline smiled at the baby in the photograph. Who could look into the face of that tiny angel and not smile? The year or more that had passed since the photo was taken made a world of difference in the child. He'd grown bigger and lost some of his babyish looks.

The next photograph on the mantel was a younger version of Stephen, and for an instant Caroline thought it was him. But this man was smiling broadly. Happy, contented, he seemed to not have a care in the world.

"This must be Joey's father," Caroline said. "Your brother."

Stephen didn't say anything. He was quiet for so long that Caroline turned away from the photographs to look at him.

"Thomas," he finally said.

Stephen rested his hand on the mantel and raised one finger as if to caress the photograph. He didn't, though. Just hovered near without actually touching it.

"Tommy…" Stephen gulped softly. "Tommy died a year ago."

A deep hurt sounded in his voice, the tiniest hint of a grave pain that stayed locked inside him. It seeped inside Caroline, filling her, making her ache, too.

"Oh, Stephen…"

"A riding accident," Stephen said, still looking at his brother's picture. A tight little smile came to his lips. "Tommy was always taking chances like that. Always living life with exuberance. Never thinking much about consequences."

"He was younger than you?" she asked, sure she'd just heard the words of a cautionary older brother.

"Four years," Stephen said. "I was twelve when our parents were killed. Tommy was eight. Uncle Colin took us in."

He uttered a short laugh. "I can't tell you the

number of times I got Tommy out of fights at school, paid his gambling debts, kept him out of trouble.''

''But that was all right with you, wasn't it?'' Caroline said.

''Of course. Tommy was young. He had a lot to learn,'' Stephen said. ''And that's what older brothers are for.''

Stephen seemed to sag under the weight of the memory, of his loss. Caroline held her breath, locked in his grief with him.

She understood the loss of a loved one. Her own mother had died. But seeing Stephen's pain—feeling it—went far beyond anything she'd experienced. She wanted to take that ache from him, ease his mind, fill that hole his brother's death had left in his heart.

Instinctively she reached for his hand resting on the mantel. But Stephen pulled away and ducked his head, lost in the past for a moment, or maybe embarrassed. He glanced at her, then without saying anything, turned and left the room. A little part of Caroline went with him.

She had tea with Delfina, then excused herself and went to Stephen's office. Richard was there and explained that Stephen had gone out unexpectedly.

Caroline spent the rest of the afternoon touring the house with Delfina and making notes of the spring cleaning that had to be done. Delfina wailed

anew in each room at how the staff had become lax
since Colin's death. Caroline had to agree.

The tour proved too much for Delfina. She retired
early and left Caroline to eat alone; Stephen still
hadn't returned. The dining room that seated twenty
was too imposing, so Caroline asked for a tray in
her room.

After spending most of the day with Delfina, she
knew how much the woman must have agonized,
deciding which bedroom to give her guest. She'd
made the decision herself, probably the first she'd
made all week.

But Caroline loved the room, with its gracefully
carved cherry furniture, thick yellow comforter,
flowered wallpaper. Situated at the back of the
house, its French doors opened to a balcony that
wrapped around much of the second floor and over-
looked the grounds.

In the adjoining bathroom and dressing room,
Caroline changed into a crisp white nightgown and
combed out her hair. She was used to sleeping in
new, different places, but an uneasiness kept her
from crawling into bed. Instead she stepped out onto
the balcony.

The stone beneath her bare feet was cool. A
breeze blew her hair around her shoulders. Caroline
stood at the wide stone railing and looked out over
the rear lawn. In the distance, lights of the city twin-
kled.

Running her hand along the stones, Caroline
strolled toward the corner of the house. Potted ferns

and flowering plants dotted the balcony, along with wicker chairs and tables. Here on the second floor, the turret wasn't part of the corner room, but was left open, forming a breezeway and allowing the balcony to wrap around the house.

As she stepped inside the turret, movement from farther down the balcony caught her eye. A little tremor of panic went through her. She hadn't expected to find anyone up at this hour, and here she was, parading around on the balcony in her nightgown.

But instead of running, Caroline stepped back into the shadows and watched. It was a man, she realized. Stephen.

French doors open behind him must lead to his bedroom, she decided. He leaned on the stone railing looking out over the grounds.

In the pale light from his bedroom, she saw that his feet were bare, contrasting with his deep blue trousers. She'd seldom seen a man's bare feet before; his were long, wide, sturdy.

The dark trousers rode low on his hips; suspenders hung useless at his sides. He wore a white sleeveless undershirt, with a scoop neck. Black hair curled over the top. As he stood in profile, Caroline saw the lines of his arm muscles, the ripples where the undershirt hugged his belly.

What was he thinking? she wondered. Staring out into the darkness, he seemed deep in thought. Was it the business meeting he'd been in all afternoon?

The fabric for Aunt Delfina's sitting room? His brother's death?

Her?

Caroline turned away. Why had she wondered such a thing? Why did she care if Stephen thought of her? Just a little?

He was a busy man. The weight of Monterey Enterprises, the house, the servants, his family was all borne on his shoulders. They were wide shoulders, yes, but surely there wasn't room left for anything—or anyone—else.

Caroline peeked around the corner again. He had so much to tend to, so many people and projects pulling at him, depending on him.

But who worried about Stephen?

Chapter Eight

"Four times. Four times in one day. Huh!"

Angus Turley's compact body was drawn so tight, Caroline thought his limbs might snap free and ping off the office walls.

Mr. Turley had been secretary at Monterey Enterprises for more years than anyone could tell Caroline, and right now, for the very first time, he was in the throes of an all-out conniption fit.

Richard was doing his best to calm him, but Mr. Turley was having none of it.

"Four times," he said again. "Four times. Just today. Mr. Monterey hasn't been into my office four times in the entire *year*. But he was four times today!"

Caroline tried to keep her head down and tend to her own work, but that was impossible in the office she now shared with Mr. Turley. A desk had been squeezed into a corner for her, and she didn't take up much room, but her presence had disturbed the flow of Mr. Turley's work, as he'd told her and was now telling Richard.

"Reorganize. That's what I'll have to do. Reorganize." Tufts of gray hair ringed the back of Mr. Turley's reddening head. "And it's all because of *her.*"

At that, Caroline's head came up. Mr. Turley glared at her. Richard tried to smile.

"All right, Mr. Turley," Richard said. "I'll—"

"That's why Mr. Monterey keeps coming in here—four times today alone! Checking up on her. Then looking over *my* work. Asking me what *I'm* doing." A vein popped out on his forehead. "Me! After years of service, he's asking me what I'm doing!"

"Mr. Turley, calm down," Richard said. "I'll handle it."

But Mr. Turley had no intention of calming down. "Women. Don't belong in the workplace. None of them."

Caroline rose from her chair. "Mr. Turley, I never intended to upset you."

His jaw tightened and the ligaments in his neck strained against his skin. "Never in all my days—"

"Come along, Caroline." Richard took her arm. "Quickly."

She hurried out of the office with Richard and breathed a sigh of relief when he closed the door behind them.

"Gracious," she said. "I've never seen a man so angry."

"I've never seen Mr. Turley angry at all." Richard shook his head. "We'll just have to find you someplace else to work."

Her first full day of employment wasn't starting off as well as she'd like. She couldn't blame Mr. Turley for his temper tantrum. Stephen had come into the office so many times this morning he'd gotten on her nerves, too. Asking questions, giving instructions he'd already given. Once he'd just stood in the doorway and looked in.

"Why don't you have some tea or something while I straighten this out," Richard said.

"I'm sorry to cause trouble."

Richard grinned. "You're worth it."

What a dear, sweet man Richard was. Caroline smiled and walked away.

On her tour of the house yesterday with Aunt Delfi, the nursery had been pointed out to Caroline, but they hadn't gone inside. Delfina seemed anxious to avoid it. Caroline wasn't, though, so with Richard busy finding her some new place to practice her chosen profession, she climbed the stairs to the second floor.

The top section of the nursery's half door stood open. Inside, Brenna sat on a stool as Joey stacked colorful wooden blocks at her feet.

"Good morning," Brenna called, and waved her inside.

Large windows let in the morning air. A big yellow sun was painted on the ceiling, with blue and white clouds fanning out around it. Clowns, carousel horses and playful animals decorated the walls.

"Hello, Joey," Caroline said.

"Joey," Brenna said, "say good morning to Miss Caroline."

He spared her a smile as he worked on stacking his blocks. "Good morning, Miss Carol."

"My goodness, this is quite a place," Caroline said, looking around the large room.

A rocking horse with a leather saddle sat in one corner beside a tiny chair with the alphabet lithographed on the back in bright letters.

"Yes, isn't it though?" Brenna said.

Rows of child-size shelves hugged two walls, holding almost every imaginable toy: a stuffed-flannel elephant mounted on wooden casters, a tin sword with a red scabbard, a policeman's hat, a wooden stable complete with horses, wagons and drivers. Surprise boxes with colorful clowns peeking out. A wind-up mechanical merry-go-round; a tin locomotive with engine, tender and two coaches.

"It looks like a toy store," Caroline said. She peered into a giant toy box crammed with a kaleidoscope, a horse-drawn fire engine, a fireman's helmet, child-size tools, wooden tops, a bright red celluloid ball.

She smiled down at Joey. "This one child plays with all of these toys?"

"Oh, this is just some of them," Brenna said. "Hardly a week goes by that something new doesn't arrive for him. Mr. Monterey is a very generous man.''

''Stephen sends all this?'' She didn't know why it surprised her, but it did.

Brenna rose from the stool and waved her arms around the room. ''This is what I allow Joey to play with. Come look.''

She opened a cupboard on the other side of the room, too high for Joey to reach. Stacked inside were a drum, a tin trumpet, a xylophone, two popguns and a paint box. Toys selected by a man who spent little time with children.

Brenna smiled. ''Nice toys, but to be played with sparingly.''

Caroline watched Joey, his tongue between his teeth, working diligently at the tower he was building. A little ache throbbed in her chest.

''To look at him, you'd never know,'' she said softly.

''About his parents, you mean?'' Brenna asked.

''So sad about his father,'' Caroline said. ''I understand his mother...left.''

''I'd worked here several months before Thomas died,'' Brenna said. ''Not long, but I saw right away how much he loved his wife. Thomas and Kellen were wild about each other. Devoted to Joey, too. Kellen was devastated when Thomas died.''

''Is that why she left?'' Caroline asked. ''Was she just too hurt to deal with Joey?''

Brenna shook her head. ''She absolutely adored Joey. In fact, when I first came to work here I didn't know why they'd even hired me. Kellen fussed over Joey constantly. After Thomas died, she and Joey were nearly inseparable. I was surprised a few weeks later when Mr. Monterey told me she'd left and wouldn't be back.''

"Did Stephen tell you why she left?''

"It wasn't Stephen," Brenna said. "His uncle, Colin. And, no, he gave no explanation.''

Caroline gazed down at the little boy kneeling on the floor. How could a mother leave her child?

"Has she come back to visit?" Caroline asked. "Or written asking about him?''

"Not a word. She moved back east somewhere with family, I understand," Brenna said. "Joey still asks about her—about both of his parents, really, but his mother especially. He has nightmares sometimes, and cries in his sleep.''

"Joey's lucky to have you," Caroline said. "Richard says you do a marvelous job caring for him.''

"Richard said that?" Color flushed her cheeks. "Really?''

Caroline nodded. "Yes, he did.''

She touched the broach at her throat. "That's… that's very kind of Mr. Paxton to notice.''

"I was in the green sitting room yesterday and I noticed Joey's mother's picture wasn't with the rest of the family," Caroline said. She'd meant to ask Stephen about it, but he'd been so upset about his brother she'd forgotten.

"Colin had all of Kellen's pictures packed

away," Brenna said. "He didn't want Joey to be upset by seeing them...or so he claimed."

"Hello there!"

Richard unlatched the half door and walked into the nursery. Joey raced to meet him.

"Uncle Richard!"

Richard swung him around and held him in his arms.

"Play with me, Uncle Richard. Please?"

"Have you been a good boy this morning?"

Joey nodded emphatically. "Oh, yes, Uncle Richard. I've been the goodest boy all morning."

"Not giving Miss Brenna a bad time, are you?"

Joey shook his head so hard his bangs bounced. "Uh-uh, Uncle Richard. I been the bestest little boy in the whole world."

Richard smiled. "Well, I can't ask for more than that, now can I?"

He sat Joey down and the boy tugged on his sleeve. "Look, I'm building a fort. Come on, Uncle Richard, you can play, too."

Richard glanced at Brenna. "Well, I don't know..."

"Please? Please?" Joey begged.

"If Miss Brenna doesn't mind," he said.

"No, of course not." She touched her hand to her hair, smoothing a few stray locks. "If you want to, that is."

"If you're sure I'm not interfering."

"If you can spare the time."

Caroline stepped between the two of them. "Of

course you're not interfering. And of course he can spare the time.''

Brenna flushed slightly and Richard tugged at his tie.

Feeling unwanted and unneeded, Caroline headed for the door. ''I have a few things to check on,'' she said, though she wasn't sure either of them was listening.

''Caroline?'' Richard called. ''I've got this situation with Mr. Turley settled. Stephen said he'd like you to come to his office.''

''Certainly,'' she said.

''Right away,'' Richard said. ''He said he'd like you to come right away. Immediately.''

At least he hadn't whistled for her like a dog. Caroline left the nursery.

Stephen was reading, slumped back in his desk chair with one ankle crossed over the other knee, when Caroline entered his office. His eyebrows were pulled together in concentration.

''Bad news? she asked.

He looked up suddenly and got to his feet, juggling the stack of papers. ''No,'' he said. Then, ''Well, yes.''

''Serious?'' she asked.

''Too early to say.'' Stephen fanned the papers, then dropped them on his desk. ''It's a report from my man Girard in Johannesburg.''

Caroline looked down at the handwritten document. ''Things aren't going well?''

''They're going well, but not as well as they

should. Girard's monthly reports have been sporadic lately. Profits are slipping.'' Stephen pulled on his ear. ''Nothing serious.''

''Did he write this report himself?'' Caroline asked.

''Yes,'' Stephen said.

''Hmm…''

''Would you care to translate that, Miss Sommerfield?''

She tapped her finger against the page. ''I think you're wise to be cautious of this man.''

He stared at the paper. ''How do you know that?''

''Because you're paying me to know that.'' Caroline gave him a smug smile. ''Richard said you wanted to see me about something?''

''No, wait a minute. I want to know why you said that about Girard.''

''It's all right here in his handwriting.'' She pointed to the words scripted on the top page of the report. ''The long, triangular crossing of the letter *T* indicates a potential for aggression and an objection to interference. The narrow spacing between words shows an intent to conceal one's true feelings.''

''So you're saying Girard resents reporting to me? He's hiding something from me?''

''I'm saying that you should be cautious of him,'' Caroline said. ''Besides, you already suspected him. Otherwise you wouldn't be upset that his reports were late and that profits were inexplicably dropping.''

''But I suspected him because I know him and

never liked him in the first place. My uncle hired him,'' Stephen said. ''You saw those traits in his handwriting without even knowing the man.''

Caroline smiled. ''That's what graphology is all about.''

''Fascinating.''

''See how smart you were to hire me?''

''A genius.'' Stephen grinned. ''Show me more of this.''

Stephen guided her to the table in the corner she'd used the night before. Her tools and the handwriting samples Richard had given her this morning were already assembled there.

''I'm working here now?'' she asked. ''In your office?''

''Temporarily. Just until we find you a permanent spot.'' He pulled out a chair for her. ''No objections, I hope?''

Dozens of them. But none she could voice.

''No,'' Caroline said, settling into the chair. ''This is fine. Temporarily.''

Stephen fetched a ball of paper from his desk drawer and uncrumpled it as he took the chair beside her.

''This is my handwriting sample from the other night,'' he said, smoothing out the sheet of paper. ''I want to know how you knew those things about me. That I am confident, enterprising and ambitious.''

''As well as pigheaded, obstinate and—''

Sexually frustrated.

Caroline pressed her lips together, holding in the words, and Stephen froze for a second. He shoved the paper toward her.

"Just explain it, would you?"

Stephen moved his chair closer until they were sitting elbow to elbow. He'd been surprised that she'd sized up Girard's personality so quickly, with just a brief glance at his handwriting. Stephen had really wanted to know more about it.

But now...

Now he was sitting with her, so close he could smell her. He could see the little flecks of gold glinting in her blue eyes. He could hear her clothing make that soft brushing sound when she moved.

Stephen pressed his lips together to keep from moaning aloud again.

Sexually frustrated. Oh, yes. If only she knew what a hornet's nest she'd uncovered.

Did she sense it now? Did she feel what he felt?

Stephen rubbed his neck. He didn't know what he was feeling, really. Plain old lust? Yes, plenty of that. His blood was already pumping faster, just because he was sitting next to her.

But there was something else, too. Something that went beyond wanting to roll around in bed with her. Stephen didn't know what it was, though, because he couldn't seem to think any further than that.

"Should we open another window?" Caroline asked. "You look—"

"I'm fine."

Stephen leaned a little closer, his handwriting

sample between them on the tabletop. Caroline studied the paper, her pretty face creased in concentration. Her bottom lip crept out slightly. His heart pumped harder.

She was sitting so close he could touch her. If he just eased forward a little he could—

Stephen stopped himself. Good thing Caroline interpreted handwriting and not thoughts. He'd get slapped again. And deserve it, again.

Enough sexual thoughts. Stephen forced himself to concentrate on the handwriting sample, on business.

"So, how do you know those…things about me?" he asked.

"Mainly by observing the length of your stem."

"My…?"

"Stem."

Stephen opened his mouth, but no words came out at first. "You noticed…?"

"Of course," Caroline said. "It's very prominent. How could I not notice? It's right there in plain sight. And very impressive. Something else I noticed was size."

Stephen stretched his neck up and shifted uncomfortably in the chair.

"Size?"

"Very important. Extremely important, actually," Caroline said. "Then there's pressure."

He ran his finger around his collar. "Pressure?"

"Heavy pressure, light pressure. One, then the

other,'' Caroline said. ''Should I demonstrate that for you? Or should we move on?''

He gulped. ''Move on.''

''Well, then, that brings us to strokes.''

Stephen groaned. He yanked loose his tie and popped open the button of his collar.

''Upstrokes, downstrokes,'' Caroline said. ''Some don't see the importance of strokes, but I do. And that, naturally, brings us to speed.''

''Naturally...'' Stephen dragged his hand over his forehead.

''Fast, then slow, then fast again,'' Caroline said. ''Which brings in rhythm. An even rhythm is best— rhythm steadily building, building, building until...release.''

Stephen slumped forward on the table.

''Release is so important, don't you think, Mr. Monterey?''

He dragged both hands down his face.

Caroline frowned at him. ''Are you certain you don't want to open another window?''

Window, hell. He needed to knock out the whole damn wall.

Caroline sat back. ''Well, that's about it. The stem of your *t* in *Monterey*, the pressure of your pen against the paper, the speed and rhythm of your pen strokes, and, of course, the release of the last letter in each word, all combine to give a complete picture of your personality. Do you have any questions, Mr. Monterey?''

Oh, yes, he had a question, all right. One big question.

But he didn't dare ask it.

Chapter Nine

Stephen remained slumped forward with his arms folded on the table. "I can't believe you gave this demonstration for the detectives at Pinkerton and they actually let you walk out of their office."

Caroline pursed her lips. "I was surprised myself."

Lucky is what she'd been, but she seemed too naive to realize it.

"So," Caroline said, stacking her papers, "I hope to find another detective agency in town I can offer my services to. Maybe one a little more progressive."

"No! You can't do that!"

She reared back. "Why are you shouting at me?"

"I'm not shouting!"

Stephen realized that he was, but couldn't help himself. Good God, what was she thinking? Parading into another detective agency with a demonstration like the one she'd just given him? He wouldn't allow it.

He tried to calm himself, tried to think of something reasonable to tell her. "You shouldn't give away all the details of how you work. If you explain everything, they won't need you."

"Oh." Caroline tilted her head. "I hadn't thought of that before. I guess you're right."

"Damn right I am."

A soft knock sounded on the open door of the office.

"Good morning," Brenna called.

Caroline suddenly realized how close Stephen sat to her, and that his tie was loose and his shirt collar open. She rose from her chair and moved away.

Brenna stepped into the office holding Joey's hand. Richard stood beside her, carrying a toy sailboat.

"Joey is on his way outside to play," Brenna said. She leaned down. "Say good morning to your uncle, Joey."

He fidgeted. "Good morning, Uncle Stephen."

Brenna spoke to him again. The child fidgeted some more, then said, "Thank you for the boat."

"We're sailing to England in the lily pond," Richard said, and ruffled the boy's hair. Joey bounced on his toes until Richard picked him up.

"I'll just get the voyage under way," Richard said, "then I'll be back."

"Take your time," Stephen said. "I'm still reading Girard's report."

Richard turned to leave, but stopped. "Oh, Steve, don't forget the meeting here today at two."

"Damn. I'd forgotten."

Richard nodded. "Do you want me to cancel it?"

"No, never mind. It's fine."

"Tell your uncle goodbye, Joey," Brenna coached.

The boy offered a brief wave as the three of them disappeared out of the office.

"Why don't you go out and play with him?" Caroline suggested. He looked as if he could use some air.

Stephen glanced up at her, buttoning his collar. "What?"

"Play," she said. "With your nephew."

He fiddled with his necktie. "I've got that report to finish, and now a meeting to prepare for. Dreshire and Morgan are a couple of barracudas. I need their warehouse and they know it."

"Don't you ever play with him?" Caroline asked.

Stephen waved away her comment and went back to his desk. With a sigh, she plucked her notebook from the table and left the office.

Walking down the hallway, she glimpsed Richard and Brenna with Joey between them. For anyone who didn't know differently, they looked like a happy little family instead of what they really were—two employees and an orphan.

Caroline made her way to the kitchen, looking over the notes she'd jotted down. She'd decided which rooms needed special attention and which needed routine cleaning. Now she had to ensure sufficient supplies were on hand to complete the tasks.

In the kitchen, Charles sprang off the stool beside a large worktable where one of the cooks was beating a bowl of batter.

"Yes, Miss Sommerfield?" he asked.

For once, the usually unflappable butler looked startled at seeing her. Caroline supposed no one from the family ventured to this end of the house very often.

The kitchen was a huge room, with multiple ovens and range tops, hanging copper pots, block worktables, and cupboards everywhere. The tile floor sparkled. A staff of three cooks moved around the room, dressed in white mobcaps and aprons.

"I'd like to see the supply closet, please," Caroline said.

Charles exchanged a glance with a large-boned, gray-haired woman, then introduced her as Mrs. Branson, the cook.

"The supply closet is down the hallway," Charles said. "But—"

"Thank you," she said.

"This way, please."

Charles led her to a large supply closet off the kitchen. Caroline consulted her notes, checked the supplies on hand and jotted down what she needed.

As she left, a little gust of morning air blew her skirt around. She looked down the narrow passageway and saw Delfina standing at the opened back door.

Delfina leaned partway out, talking in a low voice to a woman standing on the steps. Caroline couldn't get a good look at her with Delfina's considerable girth blocking most of the doorway. A faded green scarf pulled over the woman's head hid most of her face; she was wrapped in an ill-fitting, tattered sweater.

"Good morning, Delfina," Caroline called as she approached.

Delfina whirled around. The woman outside bolted.

"What's going on?" Caroline asked. "Is something wrong?"

"Wrong? *Wrong?*" Delfina worked her hands together. "Nothing's wrong. Why would something be wrong?"

Caroline peered around her, but saw no one. The woman was gone.

"Who was that?" she asked.

"No one," Delfina said. "*No one* at all. Just a beggar woman. Asking for a handout."

Caroline took one last look out the door. "I'll instruct Charles to give her something and send her on her way the next time. You shouldn't involve yourself."

"Oh, no." Delfina's chin went up slightly. "It's my duty to see to such people."

Delfina had surely picked an unexpected cause to champion, but Caroline couldn't fault her for her involvement. The Monterey family had so much, while others had so little.

"I've inventoried the supplies for spring cleaning,'' Caroline said. "We need a few more things, so I'll give the list to—"

"Fine, dear, fine. Do as you think. I've instructed Charles that you're handling the cleaning," Delfina said, and bustled away.

"Delfina?" Carolina caught up with her. "Did Stephen ask you to have Mrs. Branson prepare refreshments for his meeting this afternoon?"

"Refreshments? *Me?* I—"

"Never mind. I'll handle it," Caroline said.

Delfina mumbled something and disappeared down the hallway.

In the kitchen again, Caroline spoke with the head cook.

"No, ma'am," Mrs. Branson replied. "I've been told nothing about nothing."

Caroline thought for a moment. "Could you prepare something and have it ready at two o'clock? There will be two guests. Gentlemen. Please serve in Mr. Monterey's office."

"Did you have something special in mind?" she asked.

Caroline smiled. "Good strong coffee, laced with a little brandy. And a rum cake. Heavy on the rum."

When Caroline returned to Stephen's office, the door was closed. She knocked softly and Richard answered.

"We're going to be busy for a while," he said.

"But I'm supposed to be working on those handwriting samples you gave me this morning."

"Don't worry." Richard grinned. "Take the rest of the day off."

He disappeared into the office, and Caroline drew in a deep breath. She didn't understand what all this job fuss was about. So far, she'd been gainfully employed for a half day and hadn't done thirty minutes of work. Who could complain about that?

Still, she needed something to do. She searched out Delfina and found her in the green sitting room stretched out on the divan, surrounded by pillows, her feet up, a cloth across her forehead.

"Are you ill?" Caroline asked.

Delfina sighed. "Oh, Caroline, dear. If you only *knew.…*"

"What's wrong?" Caroline pulled a footstool over and sat beside Delfina.

"Everything.…" She sighed again. "Just *everything.*"

Delfina had the look of a woman ready to dive headlong into a slump destined to last all afternoon. But who could blame her? The family had been through a great deal in the last year or so. Thomas dying in the prime of his life, Colin passing on a few months later, then little Joey's mother abandoning him. Who could live through that heartbreak and not be affected?

Yet despite what the family had been through, Delfina was trying to go on with life, in her own way. Caroline couldn't sit by and do nothing.

She patted Delfina's hand. "Why don't we do something to cheer you up?"

Delfina rolled her eyes toward Caroline. "You *are* a dear for suggesting it. But, well…"

"I know just what we'll do," Caroline said.

Delfina heaved another sigh. "Stephen was so smart to bring you here. He's terribly smart, you know. That's why Colin gave him a free hand to run the business so long ago. But Stephen is such a worrier. Goodness, I don't know *where* he gets that."

Caroline pressed her lips together to keep from smiling. "I looked through the fabric sample book the decorator left," she said. "I picked out one you'll love. I want you to see it."

Delfina pulled the cloth from her head. "You picked one? By yourself?"

Caroline hauled the sample book from the table in the corner of the room and sat on the stool again. She flipped through the swatches.

"This one," she said.

Delfina's eyebrows rose in mild interest. "Pink?"

"Certainly," Caroline said. "Pink, for a true lady's sitting room. It will look fresh and inviting, just like you wanted. We'll get rid of this dark furniture and replace it with a lighter wood. Then we'll paint the walls a softer color, redo the paper and put white rugs on the floor."

"I—I *like* it," Delfina said. "I think."

"You'll love it," Caroline said. She gestured to the forest scene painted on the ceiling. "How about cherubs frolicking among fluffy clouds?"

Delfina sat up. "What a marvelous idea."

Caroline's heart squeezed a bit seeing the smile

on the older woman's face. "It will be such fun fixing it up."

"Well, yes, I think it would be," Delfina said. "But we'll have to wait until the decorator comes again to let him know what we've decided."

"Wait?" Caroline shook her head. "No need. We'll go to his shop."

"*Go* there? Us?"

"Certainly. Right now."

Delfina slumped again. "I don't know…"

Caroline took her hand. "I have the whole afternoon open for you and your project. Come along."

"Well…all right. If you say so, dear."

Though the trolley line ran down West Adams Boulevard, right past the Monterey home, Delfina had Charles send for the carriage, and they set out on the short journey downtown.

With the next century approaching, Los Angeles was on the verge of becoming a metropolis, growing, inching outward, stretching.

New buildings had been recently constructed, with more being developed, their skeletal frames rising everywhere. The streets were crowded with delivery wagons, horse-drawn buggies and carriages, trolley cars, eight-mule teams pulling huge oil tank wagons. Pedestrians darted for the safety of the public walkways.

Delfina surprised Caroline by talking endlessly about friends in her circle, relating gossip and a little scandal. She talked about the city, how it was growing, how it still needed to grow. Though Delfina appeared indecisive, she didn't miss a thing that went on around her.

The two of them pored over fabric samples, paint chips, colors and textures at the decorator's shop on fashionable Wilshire Boulevard. Caroline did most of the deciding, with the decorator's help. But Delfina had final approval on everything they picked out, and she liked it all.

Caroline was almost sorry when they pulled into the driveway again late in the afternoon. She'd had such a good time.

Vaguely, she wondered why it was that she'd never had a moment's fun with her own aunt Eleanor, but felt so comfortable with Stephen's aunt Delfi. Probably her own aversion to home and family, Caroline decided, climbing out of the carriage. It was so much easier to slide into someone else's family for a while, then be on her way again when the time came. She'd done it for so long it was the only thing that felt right to her.

"Well, that was certainly a day," Delfina declared as Charles greeted them in the vestibule. "Charles, some men will be arriving to begin work on the sitting room."

"Yes, ma'am," Charles said. "When shall I expect them?"

Delfina waved her hands, dismissing the whole issue. "Caroline will explain. I'm quite exhausted." She made her way to the staircase, then turned to give Caroline a final smile and wave.

"Rest well, Aunt Delfi," Caroline called. She turned to Charles. "The workmen will be here in the morning to begin renovations on the green sitting room. Please let me know when they arrive."

"Yes, ma'am," Charles said.

Caroline unpinned her hat and headed toward the rear of the house. As much fun as she'd had with Delfina, she really should accomplish some work today.

This morning, Richard had given her handwriting samples from a dozen men who worked at the Monterey warehouse complex, statements of each man's whereabouts on the night of a theft that had occurred several weeks ago. Caroline had barely begun her analysis when Mr. Turley's fit had left her without a desk, chair or place to peer through her magnifying glass.

As she approached Stephen's office, the door swung open and Stephen and Richard came out with two other men. Dreshire and Morgan, Caroline guessed, though she hadn't thought their meeting would last so long.

Dreshire and Morgan were robust men squeezed into business suits. Laughing and joking, they hardly seemed the barracudas Stephen had described earlier.

After a final round of deep male laughter, some backslapping and handshakes, Dreshire and Morgan moved on, nodding pleasantly to Caroline as they passed, then following Charles down the hallway.

"I take it the meeting went well?" Caroline asked.

Stephen and Richard exchanged broad smiles.

"I got their warehouse," Stephen announced.

Richard grinned. "And for a price you wouldn't believe."

"Good job," Stephen said to Richard, and shook his hand. "Great job. Go home. Relax. You deserve it."

"I'll have your attorney start on the paperwork in the morning," Richard said. And with a proud, satisfied smile, he left.

The pride and accomplishment the men shared spilled onto Caroline. She'd never seen Stephen smile so widely before.

"Congratulations," she said.

Stephen motioned her into the office and followed her. On a tea cart beside his desk sat a clutter of china dessert plates, cups and saucers, a silver coffee service and a few crumbs of rum cake.

"Dreshire and Morgan were more agreeable than you'd guessed?" Caroline asked.

Stephen grinned modestly. "Richard and I are both pretty good negotiators."

Caroline glanced at the empty dessert plates. "I'm sure that's what it was."

"Anyway," Stephen said, stacking up papers on his desk, "that's another situation handled."

"Richard's a tremendous help to you, isn't he?" Caroline said.

"Don't know what I'd do without him."

"Why isn't he a partner in your business?" Caroline asked. "He works hard, he's smart and I can see that you value him."

Stephen glanced up at her. "A partnership can't be simply given away."

"But he brings so much to your business."

"And I pay him very well for that," Stephen said. "Richard hasn't any financial backing, unfortunately. If he wants to improve himself, the best he can hope for is to marry well."

"Some woman whose family has money, you mean."

Stephen nodded. "Yes. A wealthy family with an ugly duckling for a daughter."

"That sounds so cold," Caroline said.

He laid his papers aside. "It is cold. But it happens all the time. The family would bankroll Richard in exchange for marrying off their daughter. The family gets a smart son-in-law who'll make them more money. Richard gets the financial footing he deserves. The daughter gets a husband. Everybody's happy."

"Except for Richard."

"And probably the daughter, eventually."

Caroline walked to the window and gazed out at the grounds. Shadows stretched across the lawn as the sun slipped toward the horizon.

"What about love?" she asked.

"Love?"

She glanced back at him. "Yes, love. You know,

when a man and woman have deep feelings for each other, feelings so deep they—''

"I know what love is," Stephen told her. "Well, I've heard, anyway."

"But it shouldn't have anything to do with marriage?" Caroline asked. "Is that what you're saying?"

Stephen walked to the window and stood beside her. They gazed out together at the side yard. Carriages rolled down the street. Pedestrians strolled past the wrought-iron fencing and low stone wall.

"Your father sent you here to find a husband. Is that why you're so set on disobeying his wishes?" Stephen asked. "You're waiting to fall in love?"

"No," Caroline said. "I just don't want to get married."

"All women want to get married."

She lifted her chin slightly. "I'm not like all women."

"I'd already noticed."

A little tingle vibrated in Caroline's stomach. She looked up at Stephen and saw that he was smiling.

He moved a little closer. "So why don't you want to get married?"

"Well…" Caroline suddenly felt as empty-headed as Aunt Delfi. All her good reasons, all the arguments she'd presented to her father before finally agreeing to the trip, all the logic that had sustained her since arriving in Los Angeles, were simply gone.

Stolen away by Stephen's closeness. His good

looks. His seductive voice. The heat that surrounded him. The trembling inside her that he caused.

"Yes?" he prompted.

But he didn't expect an answer. Couldn't want one. Not now. Not with the change she saw in his expression.

Stephen touched her arm and turned her to face him. Slowly, his fingers moved over her flesh. He lowered his head.

He kissed her.

With his mouth open. His breath hot. His lips moist.

He stole her breath. Her thoughts. Her bones.

Caroline latched on to him to keep from falling. Warmth swirled through her. He pulled her closer and she let him, helpless in his arms. Her breasts brushed his hard chest. Their thighs touched. Lost now, she kissed him back.

Stephen's heart hammered in his chest, pumping his blood faster and pushing reason further away. He struggled to hold back, to keep from devouring her, as he wanted.

Then she opened her lips.

The boldness of her invitation drove his blood faster through his heated veins. He groaned and eased his tongue inside her mouth.

Hot, sweet. Stephen pushed into this exquisite find, tasting her, losing himself in her. He crushed her against him, pushing deeper, taking more, then more, until she moaned softly.

He pulled away, startled that he'd been so blindly

consumed by her for those few moments. Stephen never lost control—of anything. Certainly not himself. Certainly not over a woman.

He eased her away just enough that he could see her face. Her cheeks were pink, her lips wet. Her blue eyes burned with passion.

He'd kissed her as if she was a two-dollar whore and he a paying customer at the tail end of a three-week dry spell.

She wasn't a whore. And his dry spell was going on two months, with no end in sight.

But how could he have lost control of himself so easily?

Stephen moved away, breaking contact with her, dissolving the aura that held them together.

"That shouldn't have happened...." His voice hoarse, his brow creased, Stephen spun around and left.

Caroline stood at the window watching him stride across the office and out the door, taking a little part of her with him. She didn't know whether to be hurt or angry.

Turning back to the window, she pressed her cheek against the cool glass, hoping it would clear her thoughts. It didn't. All she could think of was Stephen.

Stephen...and the odd realization that the woman in the green scarf standing at the fence gazing into the yard was the same woman who'd been at the back door this morning.

Chapter Ten

"Stephen? Stephen, dear?"

Delfina rushed into the breakfast room, huffing and waving the newspaper. She stopped cold in the doorway.

"Where's Stephen?"

Caroline looked up from her notebook and coffee. She'd been alone this morning since coming to the breakfast room, a cheery little room made octagonal by built-in cupboards and shelves, with a large window opening to the rear lawn. The table was set with mint green china and platters of fruits and pastries. She'd wondered the same as Delfina, but hadn't asked the cook's assistant who'd served her breakfast.

"Stephen's not been down."

"Not *down?* For breakfast?" Delfina frowned. "He's *always* down for breakfast. And I *need* him."

"What's wrong?"

Delfina sank heavily into the chair at the end of the table. "Something *dreadful* has happened."

By the way she clutched the newspaper, Caroline feared she'd read someone's obituary.

"Aunt Delfi, what is it?" she asked.

"I can't *believe* this." Delfina had drawn in a big breath, ready to launch into her story, when Stephen came into the room.

"Oh, Stephen…thank *goodness* you're here."

"Good morning, Aunt Delfi…Miss Sommerfield." He threw a glance Caroline's way without actually making eye contact with her.

Caroline's hand trembled at the sudden surge of emotion. She returned her cup to its saucer but couldn't keep it from clattering.

No one seemed to notice, thankfully, as Delfina waved the *Times* in the air.

"Stephen, this is an *emergency*," she declared.

He lowered himself into the chair at the head of the table as a servant in a gray uniform and crisp white apron poured coffee into his cup.

"What sort of emergency, Aunt Delfi?" he asked. He rubbed his eyes wearily.

Caroline chanced a look at him. When he'd first walked into the breakfast room she hadn't seen past the charcoal suit, white shirt and yellow necktie that made him look so handsome. Now she noticed that he seemed tired, as if he'd slept little. Perhaps that explained his poor selection of necktie this morning.

Absently, Caroline hoped her own appearance wasn't as bad. She'd eked out only a few hours sleep during the night herself. Stephen was probably tossing and turning over his warehouse deal. She'd lost sleep over other things, namely the kiss they'd shared yesterday afternoon.

"Stephen," Delfina said, "you need some war veterans."

That edict made his eyes open wider. Stephen stared down the table at his aunt. "I need what?"

"War veterans," Delfina said. "At least a dozen."

Stephen returned his coffee cup to the saucer without tasting a drop and swung his gaze to Caroline, silently asking for an explanation. All she could do was lift her shoulders.

"Stephen, you simply *must* find some," Delfina said.

He dragged his hand down his face as the servant placed a bowl of oatmeal at his place. "Aunt Delfi, why do I need war veterans?"

"Because of that Aurora Chalmers." Delfina thrust the newspaper toward Stephen. "It's right here on the front page. The front page, Stephen, the *front page.*"

Caroline took the newspaper and passed it along to Stephen. He scooped up a bite of oatmeal but didn't eat. He looked over the paper instead.

"Mrs. Chalmers had a reception in her home for some war veterans to recognize their sacrifices for our country," Stephen said.

"I think that's a wonderful gesture," Caroline said.

"It's *terrible,*" Delfina cried. "Don't you see? This is just the sort of thing Colin would have done here, in our home. That should be your name in the paper, Stephen, not Aurora Chalmers's.''

Stephen shook his head. ''I don't feel the need to compete with Aurora Chalmers.''

''But *Stephen*—''

''She made an admirable gesture helping our veterans and that's that,'' Stephen said. ''I see no reason to—''

''What's happening? What's *happening?*'' Panic tinged Delfina's voice as her gaze darted around the breakfast room.

Stephen sighed wearily. ''Nothing's happening, Aunt Delfi.''

''The *room* is fading,'' she wailed. ''Fading.''

''No, it's not,'' Stephen said patiently.

''It's getting darker, I tell you.'' Delfina pressed her palms against her temples. ''Darker...''

Stephen braced his elbow on the table and rested his forehead in his palm for a moment. Finally he lifted his head.

''All right, Aunt Delfi,'' he said, without any enthusiasm. ''I'll find some veterans, if that's what you want.''

''It's not what *I* want,'' she declared, her fading vision apparently restored. ''It's what we *must have*. Oh, Stephen, you know we have a position in this community.''

''Yes, Aunt Delfi, I know.'' He raised the spoon to his mouth again.

''And we must maintain that. Certain things are expected of us—of *you*.''

Stephen lowered his spoon, still not eating. "Yes, Aunt Delfi, I realize that."

"Then you must *do* something," she insisted. "We simply cannot allow our reputation to slip any further."

He dropped the spoon beside his bowl and tucked the napkin beside it. He sighed heavily and pushed himself out of the chair. "Fine, Aunt Delfi, I'll handle it."

"Oh, but Stephen, dear, what about your *breakfast?*" Delfina asked.

"I'm not hungry. I'll be in my office if you need anything else."

Stephen left the breakfast room rubbing his forehead.

"Well, thank goodness *that* crisis is handled." Delfina helped herself from a platter of pastries on the table.

Caroline had intended to have a sweet roll with her coffee, but now couldn't eat a bite. She slipped through the door and down the corridor to the kitchen.

"Have Mr. Monterey's breakfast served in his office," she said to the cook.

Mrs. Branson seemed mildly surprised but began the task as Caroline crossed the kitchen and went out the back door.

Morning sunshine was bright and warm, the air stirred by a little breeze. The weather in Los Angeles was always beautiful, just as the handbills that had drawn people from across the country had advertised. Caroline picked a jonquil blooming in the bed along the edge of the house.

She paused at the doorway, thinking of the woman in the green scarf who'd been at the back door yesterday asking for food. Caroline lingered on the steps for a moment, wondering where the woman was now.

Did she have a home? Children somewhere she was trying to feed?

Kellen Monterey flashed into her mind. Kellen, whose life was effortless here in the Monterey home, had abandoned her child so easily, while the green-scarfed woman was forced to beg to support hers.

Caroline wished she'd seen the woman's face clearly. Standing at the front fence last night, she'd been too far away for Caroline to see clearly. If the woman came around again, maybe she could do something to help.

Caroline went inside, put the flower in a bud vase and filled it with water.

"Mrs. Branson," she said. "If you see that woman out back again, let me know, please."

"What woman would that be, ma'am?"

Caroline gestured toward the back door. "The one who was here yesterday. In the green scarf."

Mrs. Branson shook her head. "Didn't see no woman yesterday."

"Well, if you should see her, let me know." Caroline placed the flower on the service cart alongside the coffee and bowl of oatmeal. "Add some fruit to the tray. The strawberries look nice this morning."

"Mr. Monterey don't prefer fruit."

"Sprinkle a little sugar on them and serve them anyway," Caroline said. "They're good for him."

Caroline ignored the cook's disapproving frown, fetched her notebook from the breakfast room and went looking for Charles.

She found him in the conservatory. He reported that the cleaning supplies she'd had him order yesterday had been delivered. Caroline gave him the list of rooms that needed the attention of the maids.

"Please ask them to begin immediately," Caroline said. "And let me know when the workmen arrive this morning."

She started to walk away, then turned back. "No need to trouble Delfina with this. Or Mr. Monterey."

"Yes, ma'am." A small smile appeared on the butler's lips. "I understand completely."

Caroline knew that he did. The servants knew more of what went on in a home than the owners did.

She supposed she'd stalled long enough.

Caroline stood in the hallway outside Stephen's office straightening her mauve skirt, flicking away little bits of lint that didn't exist. She had to go inside. She had to settle down to the work she was being paid to perform.

Not that she didn't want to work. In fact, she'd

welcome it. Something to put her mind to, to focus her thoughts on, to hold her attention. To keep her imagination from roaming.

Such passion…

Caroline closed her eyes, letting herself drift back to yesterday when Stephen had kissed her. After reliving the moment dozens of times, she still found the memory caused her heart to flutter and her stomach to tighten.

He'd kissed her with passion. Yes, she was sure that had to be it. She'd never experienced it before, but she knew. She just *knew*.

For those few brief moments he'd smothered her with it. And she'd let him. Willingly she'd been swept along, riding the rising tide of desire, need and soul-searing passion.

He'd surprised her. First with the kiss, then with its urgency. Stephen was reserved and controlled. She hadn't suspected such depths seething within him.

The power that man had over her! She'd sensed it from the first moment they'd met. Before, Caroline had feared it. She'd even refused to work for him for just that reason.

But now, after that kiss…

Caroline forced her eyes open, forced her thoughts back to the reality of her situation. She was here to do a job. Not for passionate kisses, stolen glances or romantic foolishness. Besides, she didn't want any part of that sort of thing. She wanted to be a graphologist and work for Pinkerton. So she would simply walk into the office, ignore Stephen and get to work.

With that thought firmly in her mind, Caroline went inside.

Her gaze locked on to Stephen like a gun sight to a bull's-eye. He sat hunched over his desk, reading and eating strawberries. Her heart tumbled.

Her footsteps caused him to glance up at her. He did a double take, then rose to his feet.

"Good morning," he said, and licked the tips of his fingers. "Again."

"Good morning." She pulled the cloth napkin from beneath the empty oatmeal bowl on the serving cart and passed it to him. "Again."

He looked uncomfortable and she felt uncomfortable, and she couldn't bear it, for him any more than for herself. Caroline gestured to the papers centered on his desk.

"Still working on the Johannesburg report?" she asked.

He seemed not to hear her or understand her for a moment. Then he glanced down.

"Oh, yes, the report from Girard." He wiped the napkin over his mouth and tossed it aside.

"Is the news getting any better?"

"No. It looks as if I'm going to have to do something about the situation."

"Such as?"

He shook his head. "I'm not sure. I'll have to finish the report, check out a few things, do some more investigating. I don't like to rush into things...usually.''

Caroline's skin tingled. Was their kiss yesterday something he'd rushed into? Was that what Stephen was thinking about now?

She looked away, sure she was imagining things.

''I'm going to get to work on those handwriting samples,'' she said, and gestured to the table in the corner where her tools were still laid out.

Caroline settled at the table and shuffled through the papers, trying to find where she'd left off yesterday. But the handwriting blurred. The dampness of her fingers made the papers sticky. Her trembling hands made the words jump.

And Stephen staring at her made her want to run from the room—or to him. She wasn't sure which.

She determinedly focused on her work. Stephen took his seat again and turned back to the Johannesburg report. That lasted only a few minutes before he rose and pulled open all the windows.

''You don't mind, do you?'' he asked, almost as an afterthought, waving his hand toward the windows.

''No, it's fine.'' Caroline shifted in her chair. ''Actually, I'm a little warm myself.''

''Would you like to move your table closer to the window?'' he asked.

''I don't want to be any more bother,'' she said.

''No bother.''

Stephen caught the back of her chair to assist her. She rose into the circle of his arms.

Mere inches away, Caroline gazed at him, her face upturned, his staring down. The warmth she'd felt a moment ago turned into a blazing fire.

Some inner turmoil warred within him and was reflected in the changing expressions she saw on his face. His mouth drew into a tight line; the worry lines around his eyes deepened. Then, as quickly as they'd appeared, they were gone. Stephen leaned closer.

Caroline's heart rose in her throat, thudding so hard she couldn't breathe. She rose on her tiptoes. Her eyelids sank. Her mouth sought his, guided by some unknown force. His hot breath fanned her lips, pulling her closer, closer until—

"Excuse me, Mr. Monterey."

Caroline's eyes sprang open, to find herself standing alone at the table and Stephen several feet away with his big shoulders blocking her view. She peered around him. Charles was in the doorway, glancing discreetly at everything in the room but the two of them.

"Miss Sommerfield is needed elsewhere," Charles said.

"Thank you, Charles." Caroline jetted around Stephen and out the door without looking at either man. Her heart thumped and her knees wobbled, but she made it down the hallway without collapsing.

As she'd expected, she found the five-man work crew the decorator had arranged for waiting in the green sitting room. They all looked young and strong, which Caroline was glad to see, since it was up to her to deliver the news that every piece of furniture in the sitting room had to be moved to the attic above the third floor.

The men took the news in good humor, and Caroline led the way upstairs with their first load. She thought about hoisting a chair or two onto her own back to work off some of the energy roiling through her.

Brenna and Joey came out of the nursery as she walked past.

"Good morning," she called.

Brenna took Joey's hand, but he pulled against her and whined. "Not such a good morning for us, I'm afraid."

"What's wrong?" Caroline asked. Joey didn't seem to be in the best mood today.

Brenna held tightly to his hand, keeping him out of the way of the movers, and said quietly to Caroline, "Frankly, I think he's lonely for children his own age. And he's a little bored of me. He asked about his mother again this morning."

She seemed to take it in stride and wasn't hurt.

"Aren't there some neighbor children you can visit?" Caroline asked.

Brenna rolled her eyes. "And leave the grounds? Mr. Monterey forbade it."

"Stephen?"

"No. Colin."

"But he's been dead for months."

"Change comes slowly in the Monterey household, if you hadn't noticed." Brenna gave her a long-suffering smile. "Come along, Joey."

Caroline hurried down the wide hallway to catch up with the procession of moving furniture that had gone ahead without her. She climbed the staircase to the third floor where the servants lived, then led the train of grunting men through the service door and up the final flight of steps to the attic.

Delfina had pointed out the door to her during their spring-cleaning tour, but Caroline hadn't come up here until now. The attic was nearly as big as the lower floors of the house, cut in somewhat to accommodate the steep roof, with an eight-foot, beamed ceiling. Rows of windows let in sunlight.

Half of the attic was already filled with castoffs— furniture, mirrors, boxes, crates, Joey's crib. A thin layer of dust covered everything and the air smelled musty, heavy with the scent of things discarded and forgotten.

Caroline directed the workmen where to place their burdens, but didn't leave when they headed downstairs for another load. Instead she poked around, peering into boxes, peeking into crates.

If she expected to find ghosts of the Monterey family, they weren't here. Just typical attic things. Even a wealthy family had its share of junk, it seemed.

Two huge cedar closets had been built into the attic, as was typical for homes of this type. Clothing generated by a family with position could be sizable. Evening wear was usually stored.

Caroline opened the first door and saw gowns that, judging from the waist, belonged to Delfina. Dozens in a variety of styles and colors hung there.

She opened the second closet, expecting more of the same. But Caroline stopped still in her tracks, holding open the door, staring inside.

It seemed the attic had its ghost, after all.

Chapter Eleven

Caroline pushed the closet door open wider, allowing sunlight from the windows to illuminate the interior. She became aware of the silence. No voices drifted from downstairs, no birdsongs floated in through the windows, no boards creaked beneath her feet. She stepped into the closet.

Gowns, dresses, blouses and skirts dangled from a rack on one side of the closet. Boxes stacked chest high were on the other. Shoes, slippers, boots rested on shelves at the rear.

Her lungs became labored, pulling in tight gasps of air. But it wasn't the musty smell that made it difficult for Caroline to breathe, or the warm, thick air. It was the possessions crammed into this closet, discarded, locked away and forgotten. Like the person they'd belonged to.

Caroline ran her hands over the beaded gowns, the ruffled dresses on the rack. Aunt Delfina would never fit into these things. They were a young woman's clothes. Kellen Monterey's clothes.

Everything was here, packed in hurriedly, carelessly. Shoes lay at odd angles; boxes were stacked crookedly; dresses hung awkwardly on their hangers.

Had the Monterey family been so hurt by Kellen's departure that they'd tossed her belongings here to minimize their pain? Was Kellen so traumatized over Thomas's death that she didn't care what happened to her things?

Or was it something else?

Seeing what had been left behind, Caroline knew the young woman could have taken almost nothing with her. She had good taste, judging from the cut and color of the clothing. And a tall, slender figure to set it off.

Caroline wished she knew more about Kellen Monterey, the young widow who had abandoned her son and the family she'd lived with for at least four years. According to Brenna, she never wrote, never visited. It was as if she'd died, too.

A chill caused Caroline to shiver, despite the warmth of the closet. She'd passed through other peoples' lives herself, visiting with her father while he worked at a case, then moving on. But she'd never left anything of herself behind. Had any of those people missed her? she wondered.

Caroline pried open one of the boxes and found a selection of handbags packed inside. In another she saw lace underwear and nightgowns. Hats were pushed into another.

She fingered the bow on a little straw skimmer,

feeling a strange kinship to Kellen, the woman who'd had husband, child, home and family, and left it all behind. Similar, but not the same as Caroline, who wanted none of those things to begin with.

In the final box, Caroline discovered packets of letters. Some were tied together with pink bows, others loose in the box. She slid one from beneath the ribbon and glanced over it.

As was her habit, she analyzed the writing first. Kellen's *i*'s were dotted high and to the right, indicating an outgoing attitude, extroversion and good humor. The simple bottom curve on the stroke of her lowercase *l* showed an eagerness to embrace the future. Normal spacing between lines gave the impression that she was organized and well-balanced.

Caroline read the contents of the letter. Kellen had written it to Thomas when he was away in San Francisco with Colin and Stephen for a time on some sort of business. It was filled with reports of her daily activities and everything Joey had done, down to the smallest detail. She told Thomas how she missed him, how she loved him. Caroline glanced through a few other letters; they all talked of the same things.

A warm glow burned in Caroline's stomach, then lifted into her chest until her heart ached. Kellen and Thomas had loved each other with a deep passion. Kellen had written the letters and Thomas had saved each one of them and brought them back home with him.

Deeper in the box Caroline found a stack of letters

Thomas had written to Kellen, but she couldn't bring herself to read them. What she did read was several letters from a male member of Kellen's family—brother, uncle, cousin, perhaps; Caroline couldn't determine—inviting Kellen to come see the new orange groves he'd bought. Caroline didn't recognize the name of the little town on the return address, but guessed it was in southern California, where so much citrus was grown.

There were letters from Kellen's mother, as well, written before Thomas's death. Family news, mostly. Talk of a possible trip to California. The return address indicated her mother lived in Georgia. Which was where Kellen probably was right now, Carolina decided. With her mother and not her son.

Caroline replaced the letters in the box and was about to seal it when the corner of a photograph caught her eye. It occurred to her then that among all Kellen's possessions, there wasn't one photograph of her.

Nor had she found one now. Caroline pulled the photo from the box and saw two little boys standing on steps leading to a big house. A small carpetbag sat at their feet, indicating they were leaving, or maybe arriving somewhere.

One of the boys was about twelve, the other several years younger. They were dressed in suits that fit poorly, the oldest's too small, the youngest's too large, both with patches and missing buttons.

The oldest boy was tall and thin, mostly arms and legs. His hand was clasped over the other boy's shoulder, holding him close. His face was grim, while the younger boy smiled broadly for the camera.

Caroline's heart tumbled. It was Stephen. The smaller child was Thomas. This was the photograph Stephen had mentioned to her, the one his uncle had taken when the boys arrived at his home so many years ago.

The same little worry lines Caroline had seen in Stephen's face this morning were present in the photograph. He held his brother protectively.

Yet for all the details the camera lens had captured, Caroline saw the eyes of a scared little boy trying very hard to be brave.

Caroline touched her finger to the picture, to Stephen's young, troubled face. He'd spent his whole life, it seemed, worrying and taking care of others.

She considered taking the photograph to him, thinking he might like to have the picture of him and his brother together, but changed her mind. The memory probably wasn't a happy one, and that's why the photo had been packed away.

Caroline replaced it in the box. She'd found more ghosts in the attic then she'd reckoned on.

When Caroline got down to the green sitting room again, she found Delfina wringing her hands and making little mewling sounds because, apparently, one of the workmen had asked her a question.

"Look, lady, all I want to know is if you want the draperies down or not."

Caroline stepped in, and Delfina clutched her arm like a lifeline thrown to a drowning victim.

"Oh, Caroline, this is too much. *Much* too much. We should get Stephen in here to handle this. It's simply—"

"Don't worry, Aunt Delfi, we can take care of it." Caroline patted her hand.

"We *can?*"

"Of course." Caroline turned to the workman. "Yes, please take down the drapes and all the hardware. Pack them in the boxes the decorator sent over and store them in the attic with the other things."

The man grunted, gave Delfina a withering look and went back to work.

"Caroline, oh, Caroline—" Delfina began.

"We have another project to discuss," Caroline said, guiding her out of the sitting room.

"*Another* project?"

"In the attic just now I saw several crates of books. Why are they up there?"

"Oh, that was another of Colin's fascinations," Delfina said, as they walked down the hallway. "Books, books, books. He collected them from everywhere he traveled. Some are in foreign languages. Others are rare volumes."

"Are they in good condition?"

"Oh, of course. For everyone but Colin, that is. He was *so* particular, you know. If he found a page—one single page—with the corner turned down, off it would go to the attic. Everything had to be perfect for him, or out it went."

Caroline nodded, an idea growing in her head. "I think we should donate them to the public library."

Delfina stopped. "Donate them?"

"It would be a very civic-minded gesture on the part of the Monterey family," Caroline said.

"Well…" Delfina frowned.

"The newspaper would surely want to cover it."

A smile replaced Delfina's frown. "Oh, Caroline, that's an *excellent* idea. I'll tell Stephen to—"

"No, no, there's no need to involve him. We can do it ourselves," Caroline said. "Look how well we're doing on the sitting room without him."

Delfina blinked up at her. "Well, yes, I suppose we are, aren't we."

"Of course we are," Caroline said. "Why don't you think about which room in the house you'd like to use to make the presentation."

"Yes, I can do that." Delfina headed down the hallway with a little more purpose in her walk than usual.

Running footsteps sounded behind Caroline, and Joey shot past her and headed up the staircase. Brenna came out of the breakfast room, hurrying to catch up to him. She stopped when she saw Caroline, who noted she looked a bit weary.

"Brenna, I think you and Joey both need an outing," she said.

"Probably," she agreed. "But he's a handful to take out these days. So much energy."

"I'll go with you." Caroline said the words before she'd really thought them through. But once spoken, the idea actually sounded like fun. "Yes, I'll go with you. Where would be fun to go?"

"Westlake Park is always nice. There's a lake and boats, swans and ducks. They have concerts on Sunday afternoons. It's very pretty there."

"Good. Then we'll go."

She shook her head. "I have to ask Stephen first."

Caroline had gone around him on all the other projects she'd involved herself in, but this one needed his permission. She wouldn't do anything with Joey without Stephen knowing and approving.

"We'll ask him today," Caroline said. "Come down to his office this afternoon when Joey takes his nap."

Brenna only had time to nod before she hurried up the stairs after Joey.

"Look it over. Tell me what you think."

Stephen passed the Johannesburg report across the desk to Richard.

"Problems?" Richard asked.

"Problems."

Monterey Enterprises had been involved in South Africa for nearly a decade now, chiefly in developing the infrastructure of Johannesburg and surrounding area. The corporation had interests in the country's gold and diamond fields, as well. Mining was difficult and expensive there. Political and labor problems complicated operations.

And now there were problems with Clayton Girard. Stephen sat back in his chair. The man his uncle Colin had selected to oversee their holdings had become a complication himself, it seemed.

"I'll look it over," Richard said, and fanned the pages of Girard's report.

"You know the situation over there as well as I do," Stephen said. "Better, probably."

"I'm heading over to the attorneys' office now to get them going on the warehouse purchase," Richard said, putting the report into his satchel. "I'll be back in a couple of hours."

"Good. I want that deal wrapped up." Stephen opened a ledger on top of his desk and leafed through the pages.

"How's it going with Caroline?"

The top corner of a page ripped off in Stephen's hand.

"You okay, Steve?" Richard asked.

He shoved the shredded page into the ledger and slammed it shut. "Yes, I'm fine."

Richard rose from his chair. "So, what about Caroline?"

"Nothing is going on with her. Nothing." He shoved the ledger aside.

"I meant, how is she coming on with the warehouse theft?"

"Oh." Stephen shifted in his chair. "I don't know. She's been gone this morning."

"Busy with the workmen," Richard said. "Charles mentioned it when I came in."

"Workmen? What workmen?" Stephen was a little annoyed that there were workmen in his house and he didn't know it.

"They're starting on the sitting room." Richard smiled. "I guess your aunt made her decision without you."

Aunt Delfi had begun work on the sitting room without consulting him? That was strange, but welcome news. She'd had his breakfast sent to him and refreshments served during his meeting with Dreshire and Morgan, too. He'd been surprised, and pleased, by her thoughtfulness. Maybe Aunt Delfi was pulling herself together at last.

"I'll check with Caroline," Richard said, gathering his things, "and see how she's coming on the warehouse handwriting samples."

"No," Stephen said. "Just get to the attorneys. It's more important."

Richard stood at the edge of the desk. "Have you told Caroline why she's really here? About Pickette?"

"No, and I'm not going to, either," Stephen said.

Richard shook his head, registering his disapproval of Stephen's decisions, but didn't say anything. He didn't have to.

When Richard left the office, Stephen opened another ledger but found he couldn't concentrate. Something nagged at him and he wasn't sure if it was the warehouse deal, the problem with Pickette...or the memory of his father. That, and all that came with it, never seemed to leave him alone.

But something else had him all riled up at the moment.

He and Richard seldom disagreed. It bothered him doubly that it was over Caroline.

Stephen wandered to the curio cabinet that displayed his collection of china figurines and music boxes, and peered inside. The collection always calmed him—flawless sculptures locked away in their perfect environment. He liked looking at them.

The figurine of the mother holding the baby in her arms caught his eye. It wasn't his favorite piece. He liked the tiger best. But this morning, the mother and child demanded his attention. They looked peaceful, contented.

A little shriek and a wail of laughter came in through the window. Stephen turned to see Joey race across the lawn and climb into the swing that hung from one of the shade trees. He wiggled back and forth until Brenna caught up to him and got the swing going.

Stephen braced his arm against the windowsill, watching them. They looked peaceful and contented, too.

Caroline walked into his office. Stephen smelled the scent she gave off and knew she was there before she spoke a word. He turned around. So much for peace and contentment.

"Why don't you go out and play with him?" Caroline asked, nodding through the window.

"Play with him? With Joey?" He'd never considered such a thing until Caroline had mentioned it to him once before. He gestured toward his desk. "Too much work."

"And that's close enough for you? Just watching out the window?" Caroline asked.

How did women come up with these strange questions? Where were their minds? He had a business to run, for heaven's sake.

Stephen tapped his finger on the stack of papers on his desk. "I have work," he said again.

She looked as if she wanted to say something else, but didn't. Instead, she nodded toward the table in the corner.

"I have work, too," she said.

"Good. Get on with it. I need an answer on those samples you're going over."

Caroline stopped and her chin went up. A little color touched her cheeks, and the urge to run over and kiss her surged through Stephen. Kiss her. Hold her. Run his hands over her—

"I'll get right to it, master." With a defiant little toss of her head, Caroline sat down at her table.

And for some inexplicable reason that made him want her even more.

She made a show of shuffling her papers, rearranging her magnifying glasses, scooting her chair up and back. Each movement called to Stephen, pulled at him, made his hands itch to touch her.

He gritted his teeth and flopped down in his chair. What the hell was wrong with him? Maybe he should go find himself a whore, as Richard suggested.

He looked at Caroline in her pretty pink dress, her hair done up properly, her graceful fingers holding her papers, and a whore didn't seem all that appealing. A necessity, but not an appealing one. Of course, it wouldn't take long. Not in his current condition.

Stephen grabbed another ledger from the corner of his desk. No, he decided, he wasn't going to let Caroline Sommerfield and her sweet little bottom sitting across the room from him drive him out of his own home. He had work to do. Important things to attend to. He'd simply concentrate on them and ignore her.

That decision made, he opened the ledger and began looking over the entries. But it did little to ease the ache in his chest, and nothing to relieve the pressure against his fly.

Chapter Twelve

Caroline put the finishing touches on her report, stacked the handwriting samples together and sat back in her chair.

Finished. Her first assignment as an honest-to-goodness working woman was complete.

What a tremendous sense of accomplishment she felt. Was this what men found when they worked? Was this what kept them at it?

Across the office, Stephen sat at his big desk, surrounded by important-looking reports, papers and ledgers. One day she'd have a desk of her own, Caroline thought. And a real office, too. Maybe even a secretary like Mr. Turley—well, not *exactly* like Mr. Turley—but a secretary just the same. The whole thing seemed terribly exciting.

Anxious to show Stephen that she'd completed her assignment—and found his warehouse thief—she walked to his desk. Richard had returned a short while ago and the two of them had been talking nonstop about business.

Mr. Turley had been in once, consulting with Stephen on something in a low voice. Caroline saw Mr. Turley rarely. He came and went like a phantom. Because he'd worked there for so long, and did his job so well, no one questioned him.

Caroline hadn't realized that Monterey Enterprises dealt in so many different areas until she'd heard the men talking. Stephen owned a foundry and a paint manufacturing business here in Los Angeles, not to mention the warehouse complex. He also owned oil drilling rigs, a lumber company and a shipping line. All this in addition to the Johannesburg holdings. And that's only what she'd overheard today.

All that made her handwriting analysis seem small by comparison, but didn't diminish the pride she had in her accomplishment. She had to start somewhere, and she'd just done that.

The task had been small. Certainly there were more efficient and effective ways of determining who was responsible for the theft at Stephen's warehouse. Though the Pinkerton detectives lacked vision, in Caroline's opinion, they were very knowledgeable and capable. If put on the case they could have investigated, infiltrated the warehouse crew, traced the stolen goods, done any number of things.

But instead, Stephen had chosen to give her the job and she'd done it. Caroline approached his desk, anxious to give him the good news.

Richard interrupted their conversation. "Yes, Caroline?"

She held up her report. "I found your thief."

Stephen looked up at her. "You're kidding."

"No," she said, and presented him with her report. "One Mr. Rudy Acres is the culprit."

"Well, I'll be damned," Richard said.

Stephen took the report and laid it aside, not bothering to look at it. "Are you sure?" he asked.

"As sure as the study of graphology allows me to be," Caroline said. "Mr. Acres's handwriting is very large, indicating self-absorption, concern only for himself. The straggling connections between letters shows his dislike for authority and rules. In general, your Mr. Acres is calculating and untrustworthy."

"What about the others?" Stephen asked.

"The real concern about these men is their intelligence and education." She waved the other samples she'd analyzed, still held in her hand. "Who *hired* these people?"

Richard coughed away a laugh.

Stephen cut his eyes toward her. "I did."

She should have been embarrassed by her thoughtless remark, but instead the spark in Stephen's eye caused something to flare inside her.

"In that case, Mr. Monterey, you needn't worry about further thefts." She slapped the samples down on his desk. "Because none of these men have sense enough to steal from you. I'm not sure how they even find their way to work every day."

"I don't require applicants for warehouse positions to write a review of the classics before I hire them,'' Stephen told her.

"Lucky you don't," Caroline said, "or you'd be down there hauling crates around the warehouse yourself."

"This is nothing you need to involve yourself in, Miss Sommerfield," Stephen said.

Yes, she knew that. But somehow she couldn't seem to keep from sinking elbow-deep into everything that concerned Stephen's family, Stephen's home, Stephen's business…Stephen.

"You asked me to analyze the handwriting samples and give you a report," Caroline said. "So there. That's my report."

"Thank you," he said, though at the moment he didn't seem thankful at all.

"You know, if your warehouse staff were more educated they could do a better job for you." Caroline couldn't stop herself. "You could promote men from within your organization, men who are already familiar with the operation. You could—"

"Thank you," Stephen said, ending their conversation.

He turned back to Richard, leaving Caroline standing at the desk, her head buzzing with good ideas and no one to listen to them. How rude.

She was about to tell him just that when Brenna ventured into the office.

"Excuse me? May I speak with you, Mr. Monterey?"

Richard came out of his chair so quickly he nearly

dumped the stack of papers in his lap onto the floor. He caught them in time and waved her inside.

"Come in, Miss Winslow," he breathed.

Brenna didn't wear a uniform like the rest of the servants, in an effort to soften her appearance for Joey's sake. Today she had on a cream-colored dress that brought out the brown of her eyes.

"Is something wrong with Joey?" Stephen asked.

"Joey's fine. He's napping." Brenna inclined her head toward Caroline. "We were wondering if we could take Joey for an outing to Westlake Park."

Still seated at his desk, Stephen glared up at Caroline. "No," he said, and turned back to his ledger.

Surprised by his quick answer, Brenna waited a moment before saying, "Well, thank you anyway, Mr. Monterey."

Caroline had been stunned, too. But almost instantly, she became angry.

"Why not?" she asked.

Stephen didn't bother to look up. "Because I said so."

"That's no reason."

"I don't have to give a reason."

"Yes, you do."

He looked up then. "No, I don't."

"Yes, you do!" Caroline pointed at Brenna. "She is Joey's nanny. If she thinks the child needs an outing, you should listen to her."

The line of his mouth tightened. "I know what's best for my nephew."

"Oh!" Caroline clenched her hands into fists. "You're so pigheaded!"

Stephen surged out of his chair. He snatched a sheet of paper off his desk. "Don't try to use what you've seen in my handwriting against me."

Caroline leaned closer to the desk. "I hardly need to look at your handwriting to know *that*."

"And what is that supposed to mean?"

"Anyone who has spent more than five minutes with you can see how obstinate you are."

"I am not obstinate."

"Then give me a reason why we can't take Joey for an outing," Caroline demanded.

"He doesn't need to go anywhere," Stephen told her. "He has a huge yard to play in and a nursery full of toys. He has everything a child could want right here at home."

Caroline fumed for a moment. "All right, give me another reason."

"I can give you a dozen reasons," Stephen told her. "But the most important one is that it's not safe. Two women alone is the city is troubling enough, but two women with a small child is unthinkable. I won't allow it."

"You won't let him go with us just because we're women?" Caroline asked.

"Yes."

Caroline's shoulders stiffened. "For your information, Mr. Monterey, Brenna and I are more than capable of—"

"You're not going," Stephen said. "That's final."

"Have you forgotten where I used to live?" Caroline demanded. "I crossed the Atlantic Ocean aboard a ship—alone. I traveled across the entire United States of America—alone. I'm quite sure I can make it a few miles across town to Westlake Park."

"I'm sure you can," Stephen told her. "But you're not doing it with my nephew."

"You are pigheaded." Caroline spun around, then looked back. "And that necktie looks terrible with your suit."

Caroline marched out of his office. At the doorway she glanced back to see him frowning down at his necktie.

Caroline walked off most of her anger as she headed down the hallway to where Richard and Brenna stood. They'd discreetly left Stephen's office when the shouting began.

While Caroline was still wound up, the two of them seemed to take the whole situation in stride.

"It's all right, Caroline," Brenna said. "I can keep Joey entertained here."

"But that's not the point."

"You gave it a try," Richard said. "Stephen's not known for his flexibility."

"Being obstinate and hardheaded are not qualities to be proud of," Caroline said.

Richard grinned. "Stephen knows what he wants,

and determination is required to get what you want in this world.''

''Pigheaded wretch...'' Caroline mumbled. She drew in a deep breath, calming herself. ''I'm quite determined myself.''

Richard chuckled. ''This will be a battle of wills worth watching.''

He stood with them a moment longer, then finally, reluctantly, headed off down the hallway.

''Richard is a nice man,'' Caroline said, releasing the last of her anger in a giant breath. She was always grateful for his presence. He had a calming effect on everything around him.

Brenna craned her neck, watching him disappear into Stephen's office. ''Yes...''

''You like him, don't you.''

Startled, Brenna jerked around to face Caroline. She was quiet for a moment, then shook her head. ''Richard is destined to do great things. I see it in him. But it will be difficult enough for him, given his circumstances. He'll never get anywhere with someone like me for a wife.''

Caroline knew it, too. She and Stephen had discussed it. But hearing Brenna say it, seeing the hurt in her eyes, the finality of the words, made the realization too painful.

''Maybe not,'' Caroline began.

Brenna shook her head. ''It's true. You know it. I know it. In today's society people are judged not by what they achieve, but by what they are. I'm a nanny. One of the working class. I'll never be accepted in the circles Richard needs to be a part of here in Los Angeles.''

"But if you love him—''

"It won't be enough.''

Brenna kept her chin up bravely. She'd thought this through. She knew what life was about. And life for the socially prominent was all about family lines, breeding, an acceptable background.

"I am who I am,'' Brenna said. "I can't be more than that. Not even for Richard's sake.''

"I don't like to hear you talk that way,'' Caroline said.

Brenna took Caroline's hand. "I've accepted it. You have to do the same, Caroline.''

"No, I don't.''

Brenna grinned. "You're as pigheaded as Stephen.''

"Insulting me won't change my mind,'' Caroline said, then smiled. "But look, just because Stephen said no to our outing with Joey doesn't mean it's out of the question. You and Joey both need it.''

"I don't see what we can do,'' Brenna said. "Stephen was adamant.''

"If we can't take Joey on an outing, maybe we'll bring one to him.''

"What do you mean?''

Caroline nodded firmly. "Give me a few days to work on it.''

Darkness had fallen outside Caroline's bedroom window several hours ago. She tossed in bed, comfortable under the yellow coverlet, on the eyelet-lace sheets, but still unable to sleep.

Not that she wasn't tired. She'd put in a full afternoon supervising the workmen in the soon-to-be-pink sitting room, talking with the decorator who'd come by with some last-minute suggestions and more samples to consider. She'd looked over the spring cleaning the staff was doing, ordered more supplies, all with Aunt Delfi drifting in and out, offering her unique form of help.

These and several more projects buzzed around in Caroline's head tonight, but none of them kept her from sleeping. Instead, it was a lump of sadness in her chest that left her staring at the ceiling.

Finally, she rose and tied her pale green dressing gown over her matching nightgown, and slipped out onto the balcony. The night air was still and fragrant with the flowers that bloomed in the gardens below. The stones beneath her feet were cool.

She hadn't been out here since the first night she'd stayed in the Monterey home, the night she'd found Stephen barefoot in his undershirt around the corner from the turret room. Maybe it was his habit to stand on the balcony every night, maybe not. Still, it was inappropriate to lurk in the shadows watching for him.

But tonight, impropriety didn't seem so important. And it was late, much later than when she'd glimpsed him before. He was asleep, surely.

Caroline walked silently to the turret room and peeked around the corner. No sign of Stephen. Satisfied she had the balcony to herself, Caroline ran her hand along the stone railing as she strolled, watching the streetlamps visible from this side of the house. A little breeze blew, swirling her hair around her shoulders.

The solitude of the night allowed her to sink further into thought, speculating, wishing—

A noise made her spin around. Caroline gasped as French doors opened and Stephen burst onto the balcony.

Wearing only his trousers.

Which weren't fastened.

"What the devil—Caroline?" He stopped, both hands clutching the waistband of the pants he'd yanked on. "I saw a shadow. I thought—"

The white cotton V of his underwear shone like a beacon in the darkness, capturing Caroline's gaze and freezing her in place. She'd never seen a man's underwear before—at least not while it was being worn.

Stephen glanced down to see what she was looking at, then hopped back into his room. He stepped onto the balcony a moment later, trousers buttoned, shrugging into a shirt.

"What's wrong?" he asked, coming toward her. "Are you all right? Did something happen?"

"Nothing's wrong." She turned away. Nothing except that her pulse was racing from what she'd just seen.

"Why are you out here?"

He stopped beside her. She felt the heat from his body and knew he was close.

"I just..."

She glanced back at him, and that one tiny glimpse made her turn to face him. He drew her, uncontrollably.

His hair was ruffled. Whiskers darkened his chin. He'd closed the center button on his shirt, but that was all. The tail flapped in the breeze. The cuffs were open. Black, curly hair covered his chest. His broad, strong chest.

"What are you doing out here?" Stephen asked.

Never—ever—in her entire life, in all the countries she'd lived, in all the circumstances she'd found herself, had Caroline once wanted to press her hands against a man's chest. Until now.

What did his hair feel like? Were those muscles as hard as they looked?

"Caroline, are you sure you're all right?"

She snapped out of her stupor and deliberately turned to gaze out at the yard again.

"I couldn't sleep, that's all," she said. "Sorry I disturbed you."

Stephen leaned on the stone railing beside her, looking out across the grass.

"Doesn't matter," he said. "I couldn't sleep, either."

"Why not?"

He shrugged and his shoulder brushed hers. "Business...I guess. And you?"

"I was thinking about Brenna and Richard," she

said. "And I was feeling a little sad that they love each other but can't be together."

"Richard and Brenna? In love?"

She rolled her eyes up at him. "Of course they're in love. Haven't you noticed?"

"Well, no…"

"Honestly, Stephen…" Caroline sighed. "Anyway, I think it's sad that they can't get together. I feel sorry for Brenna."

Stephen grunted. "That's strange, coming from a woman who doesn't want a husband herself."

"That doesn't mean I don't see what's good for other people."

"Are we getting back to that outing with Joey again?"

"Your pigheadedness, you mean?" she asked.

"More like yours," he said.

Caroline couldn't help smiling, just a bit. He looked down at her and smiled, too.

A wave of profound comfort washed over Caroline. Instead of Stephen making her heart pound or her temper soar, standing at his side in the evening breeze brought only contentment. A gentle easiness she'd never experienced before.

They stood there awhile in silence, and that was comfortable, too.

"Have you ever gone into the yard at night?" Caroline asked.

"Uncle Colin used to have parties there in the spring."

"No, I mean late at night when no one else is

around," Caroline said. "Taken off your shoes and felt the cool grass on your feet? Dipped your toes in the fountain?"

"I don't think I've ever considered it, let alone done it."

"Doesn't it sound like fun?"

"Not really."

She poked him playfully with her elbow. "Of course it does."

"The lawn is perfect as it is. I don't need to take off my shoes and tromp all over it to appreciate it."

"But that's not the point," Caroline said.

He gave her an if-you-say-so shrug, but didn't comment. "You never did tell me why you don't want to get married," he said after a while.

"It's because…"

"Because why?"

Caroline turned to face him then, and he turned, too. Her heart began to beat fast again and she didn't fight it, didn't try to think, didn't try to stop what was about to happen. She couldn't have stopped it, anyway.

Stephen leaned down and kissed her. Caroline curled her arms around his neck and let his lips cover hers. She rose onto tiptoes to kiss him back. Her body curved naturally into his. Softness giving way to hardness. Heat blooming between them.

She leaned her head back as his lips kissed a hot path down her cheek and settled into the valley of her neck. His hand rose along her side until his thumb brushed the base of her breast.

Caroline gasped. Stephen groaned.

He pulled away then, his breath hot and heavy against her face.

"You should never marry." Stephen's voice was hoarse and thick. "Because your husband would never get one productive thing done for all the rest of his life."

He backed away, taking the warmth with him. His gaze burned; his breath was labored. Caroline knew why. She knew what it meant.

"Go back to your room," he said.

She went.

Chapter Thirteen

The Monterey home buzzed with activity by mid-morning, but Stephen sat working in his office, ignoring it all.

Painters carrying ladders and scaffolding had trudged past the breakfast room as he ate his morning meal alone. Delfina, who usually breakfasted with him, was presumably supervising the redecorating. Stephen was pleased that she was taking over so much of the running of the house now.

He wasn't pleased that Caroline hadn't been present for breakfast. He'd wanted to see her, even if she wouldn't be wearing just her nightgown and robe.

Stephen rubbed his eyes as the columns of figures in the ledger book ran together. He'd not slept a wink after finding her on his balcony. Maybe she was tired, too. Maybe she'd slept late this morning.

Caroline in bed.

Stephen dragged both hands down his face. Good

heavens, how was he going to run his business when *this* kept happening?

A little whiff of Caroline tickled his nose and she strode briskly into his office, her lavender dress rustling, the heels of her high buttoned shoes clicking on the floor.

She didn't say anything, just fetched his suit jacket from its hanger behind the door and carried it to his desk.

"Come along, please," she said, holding the jacket.

He looked up at her. "What's going on?"

"You're needed," she said. "It won't take long."

Stephen rose and she slipped the jacket on him.

"What the devil is going on?" he asked.

"You're making a donation this morning." Caroline brushed the shoulders of his brown jacket.

"I am?"

"You are." She studied him. "Did you pick out this necktie yourself?"

He ran his hand down the blue silk. "What's wrong with it? I always pick out my own neck wear."

"So I've noticed." Caroline pressed her lips together. "Well, it's not that bad. It will do for this occasion."

"What occasion?" he asked.

"You're donating some of Uncle Colin's extensive book collection to the public library. We're having a ceremony in the blue parlor."

"A ceremony?"

"Yes. A reporter and sketch artist from the newspaper are here. Aunt Delfi is with them now."

His eyes widened. "Aunt Delfi? She's behind this?"

"There's a luncheon afterward. You don't have to stay. They understand that you have another appointment immediately after the presentation."

"I do?"

"Yes. Mr. Turley said so."

"Oh."

"Mr. Wingate is the gentleman accepting the books on behalf of the library," Caroline said. "You'll need to say something about how your uncle collected the volumes during his many travels, and how pleased you are that the community can benefit from these rare and unusual books."

A hint of a grin tugged at his lips. "I'm pleased, am I?"

She glanced up, meeting his eye for only a fraction of a second. "You are."

Caroline reached up and smoothed an errant lock of his hair. Her hand hung there for a breathless moment. Little patches of pink appeared on her cheeks as she stepped back quickly.

"Do I pass inspection, madam?" he asked.

"You'll do," she said, without looking at him again. "Come along."

Stephen followed her swaying hips out of his office and down the hallway. He would have followed her off a cliff.

In the parlor, Delfina chatted easily with the reporter and artist from the *Times,* and Mr. Wingate from the library. Caroline was pleased to see that she looked so comfortable in that setting. Aunt Delfi was an excellent hostess and had even helped arrange this morning's presentation by telephoning the newspaper herself. Delfina loved to talk on the telephone, it seemed.

Caroline's morning had been busy, overseeing the painters in the sitting room, ordering more cleaning supplies for the staff hard at work polishing the woodwork on the second floor. She'd had breakfast early and hadn't seen Stephen, which was just as well, since she knew she'd blush at the first sight of him.

After their encounter on the balcony last night, her emotions seemed almost out of control.

Standing to the side, Caroline set her mind on her task, getting it off of Stephen and his white cotton drawers, and quietly orchestrated the presentation. After Delfina had arranged for the reporter and sketch artist, Caroline had cleared Stephen's schedule with Mr. Turley, had the workmen bring down the books from the attic, and arranged them for presentation in the blue parlor. She didn't want anything to go wrong now.

Stephen made some concise, earnest remarks, and Mr. Wingate accepted the books graciously on behalf of the library. The reporter took notes, the artist sketched Stephen's likeness, and that was that. One community-minded event for the Monterey family over and done with.

"We're serving luncheon," Caroline said. Nothing like a sumptuous meal to encourage the reporter to cover future events. "I hope you gentlemen can join us."

They could, of course, and Delfina led their guests out of the parlor. When Stephen fell into step, Caroline stopped him.

"It's all right, Stephen, they know you're busy. They're not expecting you."

He glanced at the others disappearing into the hallway. "I don't mind."

"You don't like this sort of thing."

"No, not usually, but—"

"Besides, you have another appointment," she said.

"Nothing that can't wait."

"Mr. Jenkins is coming," Caroline said. "You can't keep your accountant waiting. You know how fussy he gets. And you need to wrap up this warehouse deal."

She hooked his arm in hers and guided him out of the parlor. "Run along. You have work to do."

"But—"

"And the next time you wear this suit, put on your pale yellow tie with it."

Stephen looked down at his necktie. "Yellow? Do you think so?"

"I definitely think so," she said, and left him standing in the hallway. While she wished he were still looking at his necktie, she knew his gaze followed her. She could feel it, causing her skin to tingle.

Trying to maintain a brisk and detached air around Stephen was as tiring as the tide of other emotions that always washed through her when they were together. Or when she thought of him. Or caught a glimpse of him. Or someone mentioned his name.

Caroline paused outside the dining room. No matter what, the man wore her out. She put on a smile and hurried inside.

Delfina cured Caroline's problem of seeing too much of Stephen that very afternoon. With the donation ceremony and luncheon successfully concluded, she decided Caroline should accompany her to the meeting of the Ladies Spring Flower Club. The organization of women dedicated themselves to beautifying the city of Los Angeles by sharing knowledge and gardening skills.

"You'll enjoy this meeting," Delfina predicted as they climbed into the carriage. "All the best families are represented."

"Are you sure I should come?" Caroline asked.

"Of course!" Delfina beamed. "I *must* show off my connection with the royalty of Europe. Besides, Aurora Chalmers will be there and I want to make sure she watches the *Times* for our *library* donation."

Although it didn't sit quite right with her, Caroline couldn't argue. She'd arranged the donation to satisfy what Delfina saw as the slumping position of the Monterey family, and because the library really could use the books.

"Now, *tell* me, dear," Delfina said. "What sort of event should we plan next?"

"I do have something in mind," Caroline said.

"Honoring our veterans, perhaps?"

She shook her head. "No, but something just as worthy."

"It *must* be worthy of the Monterey name," Delfina insisted.

"It will be," Caroline assured her.

"Shall we get to work on it when we return home?"

Caroline knew Delfina's "we" really meant *her*. But that suited Caroline fine. Delfi did as much as she could. Caroline didn't expect any more of her.

She smiled across the carriage at the older woman. "We should definitely get right on it. We'll want to have this event within the next few days. In fact, we might even make it an annual event."

Delfina sighed dreamily. "An annual Monterey event. How *delightful*."

And delightful was how Caroline felt about the meeting of the Ladies Spring Flower Club. The women welcomed her warmly and were anxious to hear about her life in Europe. A few of the other women had visited some of the same homes that Caroline and her father had been guests in. One of them had even heard of the renowned Jacob Jackson

Sommerfield, and regaled the other women with tales of his extraordinary detective work.

Delfina basked in the glory of the excitement Caroline brought to the day's club meeting. Even Aurora Chalmers had been impressed, and even more pleasing, speechless.

On the heels of that success, Delfina brought Caroline to meetings of the Christian Women's Charity Club and the Ladies Music Circle during the next week. She also went to three teas and a luncheon.

Delfina decided to have a tea and two luncheons of her own, which Caroline organized. Caroline discreetly got the names of several of Stephen's business associates from Richard and invited their wives, along with Delfina's other guests. It couldn't hurt, she thought.

If Stephen noticed that Caroline wasn't working at her paid profession in his office every day, he didn't mention it. The few times she had ventured inside, both he and Richard had their heads together, deep in a serious discussion. From the fragments of conversation she caught, it concerned Clayton Girard in Johannesburg, not surprisingly.

But not a night went by that Caroline didn't consider venturing onto the balcony again. Images of Stephen waiting there in the darkness pulled her toward the French doors of her bedroom. He'd kissed her. Touched her. And they'd talked the comfortable talk of good friends. She didn't leave her room, though, and wasn't sure why.

Returning home from a luncheon, Delfina chattered on and on about what Emily Waterson had just served, what china pattern she'd served from.

"We certainly can't make *that* mistake," Delfina declared.

Caroline smiled kindly at Delfina and her small world. Sometimes she worried what would happen to the woman if she were forced to make a serious decision, or was faced with an actual crisis. She shuddered to think.

The carriage came to a stop in front of the Monterey home and the driver opened the door for them. Although the trolley line that criss-crossed the city ran right down West Adams Boulevard, Stephen insisted his aunt take the carriage when she needed to go out. Caroline had thought it silly at first, but she'd grown accustomed to the driver and the comfort of the carriage.

Stepping outside, Caroline was surprised to see a wagon sitting in the driveway. Probably red at one time, the paint was faded and peeling now. A team of workhorses was hitched to it. A woman in a gingham dress and straw bonnet sat on the seat, and crowded in the back were eight children. The youngest had his thumb plugged into his mouth, and the oldest was a long-limbed, gangly boy on the verge of manhood.

The family looked as if they'd been sitting there for a while, all crammed into the wagon. Some of the younger children whined. The afternoon was hot and they all looked wilted.

"Good afternoon," Caroline called.

The woman fingered the coarse fabric of her skirt

and smiled shyly. "Good afternoon to you, ma'am. My husband is inside talking with Mr. Monterey. We don't mean no trouble."

"Of course not," Caroline said, and thought it odd the woman would say such a thing.

Charles met Caroline in the vestibule, and as Delfina breezed past and up the stairs, Caroline asked, "Charles, who are those people?"

"A meeting is taking place with Mr. Monterey," he said.

"Why weren't they invited inside?"

Charles pinched his lips together. "Mr. Monterey didn't invite them."

"How long have they been sitting out there?"

"Thirty minutes, perhaps."

Caroline planted her hand on her hip. "Good gracious, Charles, offer them some refreshment."

His lips pinched tighter. "I don't think Mr. Monterey would approve."

"It's hot out there. Those are children."

"But madam, if I could be permitted—"

"Please, Charles, take them something at once."

"As you wish, madam," Charles said, and disappeared down the hallway.

Caroline deposited her handbag on the table in the vestibule and went outside again just as Charles reappeared with a tray of frosty lemonades. Eight sets of little hands reached for the glasses, chattering excitedly. The woman accepted hers more cautiously, but drank it down quickly.

"You kids thank this nice lady, now, you hear?" she said to her children.

A chorus of thank-yous rose from the rear of the wagon and brought a smile to Caroline's face.

"Are you in town on business?" Caroline asked.

The woman nodded. "My husband is taking care of our business. We brought the kids along 'cause they don't get to see the city too often."

"Where are you from?"

"We got us a fine place down around Riverside." The woman smiled proudly. "My husband, he works the land hard. My young 'uns work just as hard."

The woman turned her attention to the front door. "Here comes my husband now."

A man in worn clothing pulled a battered hat on his head and hurried down the front steps. Stephen stood in the vestibule, blocking the doorway, rigid and tense and glaring at them all.

In all the time she'd known him, Stephen had kept a tight rein on his emotions. He'd never lost his temper, never raised his voice, even when they'd argued over Joey's outing. But he was angry now. He was beyond angry.

He saw the lemonade glasses, then swung his gaze to Caroline, and though she hadn't thought it possible, his anger deepened. She read it in the swell of his chest, the stiffening of his stance, the squaring of his shoulders.

Caroline turned back to the woman. "I'm sorry, I didn't get your name."

The woman looked at her husband, at Stephen, then back at Caroline.

"Pickette," she said. "Mrs. Russell Pickette."

Chapter Fourteen

Stephen stalked back into the house. Caroline left Charles to gather the lemonade glasses, and hurried inside after him.

"Stephen?" she called to his wide back as he strode down the hallway. He heard her—he had to have—but didn't stop. Caroline picked up her skirt and hurried after him.

When she reached his office door she found him pacing in front of the windows, staring at the floor, slamming his fist into his open palm. Richard appeared beside her and touched her arm.

"Don't, Caroline," he said. "Stephen's upset. He needs some time. He needs to be alone."

"No, he doesn't." She pushed past him into the office. She was halfway into the room when Stephen rounded, stopping her in her tracks. Fierce anger radiated from him and it was directed at her—some of it, anyway. Still, Caroline wasn't frightened of him.

"What in blazes did you think you were doing?" Stephen pointed through the house toward the front driveway. "Those people didn't deserve one ounce of hospitality! Not a cent's worth! Not of my money!"

He stomped over to her, towering over her, crowding her. "You had no business interfering. It was none of your concern."

Caroline stood very still, not giving an inch. She tilted her face up toward his angry one and said softly, "They were children, Stephen."

His anger deflated then, dissipated like hot air from a balloon. His shoulders sagged and he turned away.

"That's not the point," he said. He walked to the window and braced his arms on the sill, staring out.

"It's not the lemonade, it's something else, " Caroline said. "What is it, Stephen? Who are those people?"

He pushed his hand through his hair and pulled at his collar, refusing to turn and face her.

"Nobody," he finally said. "They're not important. It's just business."

She walked closer and stood near him at the window. Gazing out at his neat, orderly rear lawn seemed to calm him, the same as when he stared into his curio cabinet of china figurines and music boxes. His anger was still evident in the tight lines of his face, though under control now. But there was something else, too. Something deeper.

Caroline reached for his arm. At her touch, Stephen jerked away and strode back to his desk. He picked up some papers and looked them over, though she was certain he didn't see a word that was written there.

"As I said, Caroline, it's just business. Nothing you should concern yourself with."

"Liar."

He cut his gaze over to her, opened his mouth, then closed it again, shutting off the words and emotions that threatened to spill out with them.

Stephen gestured with the papers in his hand. "If you'll excuse me, I have work to do."

"You can tell me, you know," she said gently. "Actually speaking your feelings aloud won't do irrevocable harm."

Stephen turned away, studied the papers in his hand again. "This is a business matter. I have no feelings about it."

Here was a battle she wouldn't win. Not today, anyway.

"Fine," Caroline said, and left the office.

"Stephen's gone? Gone where?"

Caroline stood in front of Stephen's desk, but it was Richard who sat behind it this morning.

"Downtown. The Bradbury Building," Richard said. "He's signing papers for the new warehouse and handling a few other things."

"But he's supposed to be here," Caroline said. "Mr. Turley said so."

Richard sat back in the chair. "What's going on?"

She huffed impatiently. The next Monterey event—the one destined to become an annual occurrence—was taking place this afternoon. Stephen was supposed to be home all afternoon, according to Mr. Turley. She'd made sure his schedule was clear so that she could have him make an appearance for the newspaper reporter.

"There's another community event," Caroline explained.

Richard glanced out the window behind him at the staff busy setting up tables on the back lawn. "Yes, I see something's going on. I don't know what's got into Delfina, but she's certainly taken hold of things lately."

"Unfortunately, it will be for naught if Stephen doesn't show up," Caroline said. "Do you know when he'll be back?"

Richard shook his head. "No, not really. I was supposed to handle this, but at the last minute he wanted to do it himself."

"He's still upset about yesterday, isn't he?" Caroline asked. "Who were those people, Richard? Why did they get him so angry?"

He rose and gathered up some papers. "You'll have to discuss that with Stephen, Caroline."

"But he won't talk about it."

"I can't, either," Richard said. "In the meantime, I've got some handwriting samples for you to look at."

"Now?"

Richard grinned. "Jobs can be so inconvenient sometimes, can't they?"

Caroline took the papers he held out to her. "What's this all about?"

"Stephen was quite impressed when you pointed out who the likely thief was at the warehouse," Richard said. "He shared that with other business-men and they've asked you to look at some of their employees."

"Really?" Surprised, she looked at the papers, then up at Richard again. "Stephen recommended me? Really?"

"He did."

Richard didn't seem as pleased by it as she was, but Caroline wasn't about to let this small advance-ment go unappreciated.

"How sweet of him," Caroline said, smiling. "I had no idea he thought so much of my work that he would give me a recommendation to others."

Richard grunted and dropped into the chair again, shuffling papers. "If you could get working on those, Stephen would appreciate it."

"Of course."

"Oh, by the way, Stephen hired a Pinkerton man to keep an eye on Rudy Acres."

"The warehouse thief?"

"Yes. If he's the one responsible, as you sug-gested, the agent will catch him in the act and send him off to jail."

Caroline faltered. "Jail?"

''Of course, jail. What did you think we'd do with him?'' Richard asked.

''I—I don't know....''

Caroline sat in her chair at her little table in her corner of the office. A man might go to jail. Because of her.

Looking at handwriting samples, matching up strokes and stems and letter endings to personality traits, was fascinating work. The scope of a living, breathing human being spread out in a few lines of handwriting, just waiting to be deciphered. She'd done it at parties for fun, and as exercises for her tutors in Europe.

But she'd never sent a man to jail with it before.

Caroline sorted through the handwriting samples Richard had given her. She arranged her magnifying glasses, took out fresh paper for notes, tested her pencil. But she couldn't bring herself to begin work.

''These samples,'' she said to Richard. ''They're suspected of stealing also?''

''You mean the men who wrote them?''

A lump of something sour rose in Caroline's throat. ''Yes, the men who wrote them.''

He nodded. ''Theft is what Stephen told me.''

Caroline's fingers grew damp as she handled the samples. Would she send one of these men to jail, too? Which one? Whose life would she ruin? Whose family would be left without a husband, father, son?

Richard went back to his work. Caroline couldn't. She tried, but she couldn't.

Finally, she gave up.

"I really have to check on things for this afternoon's event," she said, rising from the table.

He looked across the desk at her. "Something's wrong. What is it?"

"Nothing," she said quickly. "I just…"

"Just what?"

Caroline shook her head. "Tell Stephen I'll get right on them in the morning."

She left the samples and the office without a backward look.

When Stephen stepped into the vestibule, the familiar peace and tranquility of his home overtook him, leaving the heat, the traffic, the noises of the city outside where they belonged. He loved his neat, orderly house, which seemed to shine a little brighter in the past few days and smell a little sweeter. He loved his office, the concise stacks of work on his desk, the supplies arranged just so inside the drawers.

And even though Charles was nowhere to be seen at the moment—which was odd—that didn't diminish Stephen's pleasure at arriving home. He dropped his derby on the table in the vestibule and carried his satchel back to his office.

Everything had gone smoothly at his attorney's office today. The warehouse was his, legally, bought and paid for, and he was anxious to share the news with Richard.

But Richard wasn't in the office. Stephen dropped his satchel on the desk and thought for a moment, but couldn't remember anyplace Richard was going. He was supposed to be here. In fact, they were going to spend the afternoon—

Stephen's stomach bottomed out, then sprang into his chest. He went to the window. Outside, on his back lawn, were—children. Tiny little children.

Dozens of them. Running, jumping, tumbling in the grass. Swarming like ants. And they were in his backyard!

Stephen rushed to the rear entrance of the house and out onto the steps, to be met with laughter, giggling, squeals. Clowns, pony rides, balloons. Tables with red checkered cloths piled with food remains and half-empty glasses.

"Stephen, dear, there you *are*."

Aunt Delfi levered herself out of a chair at one of the tables and came to greet him.

"Isn't this *wonderful?*" she declared.

Mouth sagging, he turned to her. "What the—"

"Caroline and I decided—"

"Caroline?"

He spun around until he spotted her near a makeshift wire pen holding a rabbit, a hen, two piglets and a goat. He charged across the yard, dodging children darting across his path.

"Stephen, you're here." She rose from talking to a little girl with blond curls in a plain brown pinafore. "I was afraid you wouldn't make it."

He plastered his hand against his forehead. "What the hell—"

"Stephen, your language." Caroline bobbed her

eyebrows and tilted her head toward two nuns supervising the pony ride.

"These are *children*...."

Caroline gazed around the yard. "Yes?"

"They're *here*. On my *lawn*. My perfect lawn."

"The lawn is still perfect, Stephen. It just has children on it now."

"Where the hell did they come from?"

"Shh!" Caroline grasped his arm. "You'd better come sit down. You don't look well."

She led him to a bench in the shade of an oak.

"There're so many of them," he said.

"Twelve," Caroline said.

"That's all? Twelve?" He looked again. "No, there's more. I'm sure of it. Count them again. Some might have slipped in under the fence."

He paced for a moment, then Caroline took his arm again and he sat down on the bench.

"Everything is fine, Stephen," she said, sitting beside him. "We have plenty of supervision for the children. See? Three nuns—"

"What the hell do nuns know about children?"

She patted his arm. "They run the Sacred Heart Orphanage."

Stephen stopped and looked out over the yard again. "These are orphans?"

Caroline nodded.

"All these children?"

"Yes, they are."

"I didn't know...." Stephen looked at the children running in his yard again, realizing for the first time that they were all dressed alike. Girls in brown pinafores, boys in brown knee pants and white shirts. "What are they doing here?"

"It's another Monterey public image event," Caroline said. "There's a reporter and a sketch artist from the newspaper here somewhere."

"Aunt Delfi did all of this?" Stephen asked.

"She's considering making it an annual event," Caroline said.

Stephen rose and slid his hands into his trouser pockets, looking out over the children playing on the lawn.

"They're so young," he said.

Caroline got up from the bench. "We asked the sisters to bring children who were around the same age as Joey, so he could enjoy the day, too."

He spotted Joey across the lawn with three other little boys, having a sword fight with sticks.

Stephen smiled. "Tommy and I used to do that...."

"Would you like to go meet the children?" Caroline asked.

Allowing Caroline to take the lead, Stephen waded into the mass of tiny, wiggly bodies.

"It's not that I don't like children...exactly," Stephen said. And that was true. He did like children, albeit from a distance.

"I know," she said, and smiled up at him. "You certainly give Joey everything on this earth he could possibly want—materially speaking, of course."

She stopped to talk to a little boy who was holding a cookie in each hand and whose cheeks were puffed out with at least two more. It occurred to Stephen how pretty Caroline looked today, wearing a mint green dress and a straw hat with a wide brim and orange, white and green ribbons on the crown.

He thought she always looked pretty. But today, right now, kneeling down helping the child with his cookies, getting crumbs on her skirt, she looked especially pretty.

They walked across the lawn together. Richard and Brenna were helping at the petting farm. Caroline scooped the bunny from the wire pen and held it for a little girl too frightened to do it herself. Gently she took the child's hand and helped her stroke the rabbit's soft fur. Caroline's face lit up when the little girl smiled.

As they made their way through the yard, Caroline never hesitated to stop and talk with any of the children, wipe a dirty mouth, clean a sticky hand, listen or offer a hug.

"It's all right for you to talk to them," Caroline said.

Stephen forced a small laugh. "I guess they don't bite, do they?"

"Well, they might." Caroline grinned.

He put his hands in his pockets again and kept walking.

Delfina kept the reporter entertained until Stephen and Caroline found them in the crowd and Stephen made some appropriate comments about the events of the day. The artist, who had already sketched several scenes in his notebook, drew one of Stephen before he and the reporter announced they had all they needed for the story and left.

Caroline helped with the ice cream. Servants were there to oversee the children, but Caroline couldn't seem to detach herself from them. It was a side of her Stephen hadn't seen before.

After all the children were served, Caroline sat with Stephen and called Richard and Brenna to join them, and they ate ice cream together.

"Caroline, this is a wonderful day," Brenna said. "The children are having a marvelous time."

"Yes, they are." Caroline's smile faded. "But seeing them breaks my heart. They have so little."

"Maybe we should do this more often?" Richard suggested.

"That would be so nice," Brenna agreed.

Stephen bristled. "We'll have to think about that."

"Joey's having a delightful time," Brenna said.

They all turned to see him seated at the table, talking nonstop to the little boys around him.

"He didn't even want to stop for ice cream," Brenna said.

"It's good for him," Richard said, "being around boys his own age."

Stephen paused in midbite as the others stared at him. He lowered his spoon.

"I'm not changing my mind about you two taking him to the park, if that's what you're thinking," he said.

"But Stephen, an occasional change in his routine is so good for him," Caroline said. "Isn't that right, Brenna?"

She nodded. "A child needs exposure to different situations."

"I'm not disagreeing with that," Stephen said. "My concern is for two women alone, responsible for the boy for a whole day."

"Stephen—"

"I'll go with them."

They turned to Richard, not sure it was he who had spoken. He shifted, then said, a little louder this time, "I'll go with them."

"You will?" Caroline asked.

Richard glanced at Brenna. "If you have no objections, that is."

She dipped her lashes. "If you're sure you'd like to go."

"As long as you don't mind."

"If it's not too much of a bother for you."

"I don't want to inter—"

"It's all set," Caroline declared. "The three of us will take Joey to the park on Sunday."

"Is that all right with you?" Brenna asked Stephen.

He paused with his spoon halfway to his mouth, and a little boy raced by, jarring his elbow. Strawberry ice cream splattered onto his shirt and necktie.

Stephen frowned, concerned about his clothing rather than the child who'd caused the damage.

"Damn," he mumbled, picking up a napkin. "This was my favorite necktie."

"*That?*" Caroline leaned forward, her eyes wide.

"What's wrong with it?" Richard asked.

"Yes," Stephen said, "what's wrong with it?"

Brenna made a little clucking sound and Caroline rolled her eyes.

"It's ugly, Stephen," Caroline said.

"No, it's not." Stephen looked down at his necktie, then up at Caroline again. "Is it?"

Caroline and Brenna both nodded. Richard shrugged helplessly, then asked, "Why don't you come with us on Sunday, Steve?"

Wiping his necktie with his napkin, Stephen shook his head. "Too much work. This Johannesburg situation has to be resolved, one way or the other."

Richard saluted Caroline and Brenna with a spoon of strawberry ice cream. "Ladies, Sunday it is."

Bone weary, Caroline crawled into bed and pulled the coverlet over her. Her head sank into the feather pillows and she closed her eyes.

Visions of girls and boys filled her head. The day had been a success, by anyone's standards. Caroline had hated to see the orphans leave. Little pieces of her heart went with each of them. It was a strange reaction. She'd been around children before but had never felt this way.

It was so sad for a child to lose a parent. But both? At such a young age? Her mother had died long ago, but she'd had her father, and the two of them had been a family. He'd carried on and made a good life for them.

But what if it had been the other parent she'd lost? Caroline thought for a moment how differently her life might have turned out. How many children were orphaned because their mothers simply didn't have the money necessary to care for them? Without a husband, a woman had few ways of supporting a family. There weren't many respectable jobs a woman could hold down. And most of those paid very little.

What about women who were too sick to work? Too proud to come to places like the Monterey home and ask for a handout at the back door?

Caroline thought again of the green-scarfed woman. She'd gotten only a vague impression of the woman's features, but she'd recognized the envy in her expression as she stood at the fence and gazed into the yard. A deep longing for something she couldn't have, something just out of her reach.

Today wasn't enough, Caroline decided. This Monterey event would have to come round much more often than annually.

A knock sounded, faint and tentative. Caroline sat up. It hadn't come from the door, but across the room. A shadow darkened the French doors leading to the balcony.

Her heart thudded against her ribs. It was Stephen.

Chapter Fifteen

Caroline slipped on her dressing gown and tied the sash around her waist. The shadow outside the French doors was tall, hulking. Stephen, for sure.

She didn't take the time to wonder what he wanted, why he was here. Her thoughts spun too quickly for that. She opened the door.

Stephen towered over her in the doorway, his features intense in the dim light. He wore a white shirt, opened at the neck, and trousers—fastened.

"Is something wrong?" she asked.

"No, I, ah…" His gaze dropped to her feet, then rose quickly, taking in the length of her. "Did I wake you?"

Caroline pushed her hair back off her shoulder, conscious of her state of dress, the darkness, their isolation. When she'd met him on the balcony on previous nights it had been by chance. This was by design.

"No," Caroline said, "I'd just gotten into—"

Bed.

Her cheeks burned, sending a sizzle down her body. It arced to Stephen, causing him to draw in a big breath.

"I didn't come to the door," Stephen said, "because I didn't want anyone to see and get the wrong idea."

He cleared his throat and backed up a few steps. "I want to talk to you."

Caroline followed him onto the balcony, more comfortable here than in the confined space of her bedroom; Stephen seemed to shrink every room he entered. She rested her arms on the stone railing and let the cool evening breeze fan her face and tug at her hair.

Beside her, Stephen did the same. Together they looked out over the lawn, at the lights of downtown businesses off in the distance, a few glowing windows in neighboring houses. After a few moments, she sensed him relax.

"I guess my lawn will recover." He uttered a short laugh. "Looks like I'll pull through, too."

Caroline smiled. "Then I'd say the day was definitely a success."

"I'm not all that comfortable around children."

"They're messy," Caroline agreed. "Clumsy, thoughtless, awkward—the list is endless, ever changing as they grow."

"It's not that." Stephen touched his hand to his chest and said softly, "Childhood hurts."

He was talking about his own childhood. Emotion

swelled in Caroline until her chest hurt, too. She wanted to reach out to him but knew he'd back away. She didn't want to lose this moment with him.

"Your childhood hurt," she said. "Seeing those children today reminded you."

Stephen was quiet for a moment. "I was twelve when my parents died. Thomas was eight. We weren't sent to an orphanage, just shuffled around for a while until Uncle Colin agreed to take us."

"That must have been awful," Caroline said. At least when her mother died, her routine hadn't changed. Her father had been there, comforting and supporting her.

"Uncle Colin had our photograph taken the afternoon we arrived at his home," Stephen reminded her. He looked away. "So we wouldn't forget, he said."

It was the photograph she'd found among Kellen's belongings in the attic. The boys in their threadbare, ill-fitting clothing. Thomas, younger, appeared thrilled at arriving at their new home. Stephen had carried the burden of the truth for the both of them.

"Didn't your uncle want you and your brother?" Caroline asked.

"He did. I'm certain he did," Stephen said. "But there was always that…something…."

Caroline couldn't stand it another moment. Desperate to comfort him, to ease the worry lines in his face, she reached out and touched Stephen's forearm. And as she knew would happen, he pulled away.

Stephen straightened and drew in a deep breath, casting off his mood and changing the subject.

"There's something I need to talk to you about, Caroline."

Her heart ached. She didn't want to talk about anything but Stephen and what he'd been through. She wanted to know everything about him. She wanted to crawl inside him and know him as well as she knew herself.

He pulled her in that way. She'd felt it before. Right from the very beginning he'd had the power to do that to her.

Stephen Monterey devoured her. Smothered her. Took over her mind, her thoughts, controlled her actions in an indirect way.

At first, Caroline had been frightened of it. She'd tried to run, ignore him, go on with her own life. She hadn't been able to. Something about Stephen wouldn't let her.

"It's about your employment here," Stephen said.

His words jarred her from her thoughts, reminding her of all the times she'd spent with Delfina instead of working.

"Have I done something wrong?" she asked.

"Yes, in a way." Stephen leaned an elbow on the stone railing so he wasn't quite so tall. "Richard told me you seemed upset today that I'd alerted a

Pinkerton detective to our theft suspect, and that he might to go jail.''

''Yes. Mr. Acres.'' Caroline glanced down at her hands resting on the stones. Richard, such a dear man, had noticed her concern and passed it along to Stephen. But what did he think? That she was silly? Stupid?

''I don't want you to worry over what's happened,'' Stephen said gently. ''You should be proud of what you've done.''

''Proud? That I've possibly sent a man to jail?''

''That you've accomplished what you set out to accomplish,'' Stephen said. ''You had a job to do and you did it.''

''But, Stephen, jail…''

''You have an extraordinary skill, Caroline. It's not your fault you caught a thief—it's the thief's fault for having stolen in the first place.''

She gazed up at him. ''Do you think so?''

''Actions have consequences,'' Stephen said. ''Rudy Acres, if he's the guilty party, made his own problems when he decided to commit the thefts. He has to pay for what he's done.''

''I can't help feeling responsible, somehow.''

Stephen touched her shoulder, turning her to face him. ''You did the right thing, Caroline. And no one should ever feel bad for doing the right thing.''

Her insides warmed, melting away the guilt she felt over naming Rudy Acres as the prime suspect.

Caroline smiled up at him. ''Thank you for saying that.''

He gave her a quick nod. "You shouldn't waste a moment's concern on the likes of Rudy Acres. And if it turns out that you're right and he's the thief, don't be afraid that he'll retaliate in any way. He's a penny-ante crook and no real threat."

She gasped. "He might do that? Try and get back at me?"

"Didn't I just say not to worry?" Stephen admonished. "He doesn't know who you are, Caroline, or that you're in any way responsible. You're in no danger."

"But what about you?"

Stephen shrugged off her concern. "I'm not the least bit concerned over the Rudy Acreses of the world."

"Well, if you're sure."

"I'm very sure."

He was so sure, so confident, that Caroline believed him completely.

"All right, then, I'll get at those new handwriting samples in the morning," she said.

"Let me take care of the consequences," Stephen said.

A few minutes passed, but he didn't release her arm. And she didn't want him to. She wanted him to kiss her.

The notion that she'd somehow, in a few weeks time, turned into a shameless, wanton woman didn't really bother her. She wasn't shameless about every man who came along. Only Stephen.

Standing on the balcony, close enough to feel his

warmth, Caroline thought she'd scream if he didn't kiss her. Stephen looked as if he'd explode if it didn't happen.

He leaned his head down. Shameless, wanton woman that she'd become, Caroline rose on her toes.

And stopped when a knock sounded from inside her room.

They both stopped, inches—agonizing inches—apart.

Stephen pulled away and released her.

"I—I should see who that is." She waved her hand toward her bedroom.

"You should." Stephen shifted from foot to foot. "Well, goodnight."

"Goodnight," she said softly. "Stephen?"

He turned back.

"Thank you for talking to me tonight about Rudy Acres. You made me feel much better."

"You're far too beautiful for worry lines, Caroline," he said softly, then disappeared down the balcony.

Caroline floated back into her bedroom, doubting that her feet would ever touch the ground again. She switched on the lamp at her bedside and opened the door. Brenna waited in the hallway, wearing her dressing gown.

She glanced up and down the corridor. "Could we talk?"

"Of course." Caroline let her in and closed the door behind her. She offered Brenna a seat on the overstuffed chair in the corner, but she refused.

"I don't mean to disturb you," Brenna said, twisting her fingers together. "I know it's late."

"It's all right. I wasn't sleeping, anyway." Without wanting to, Caroline's gaze darted to the French doors and the balcony beyond. "And I doubt I'll get any sleep tonight."

"All the excitement."

Caroline's cheeks flushed. Did Brenna know?

"With the children here," Brenna explained.

"Oh, yes, of course. The children." Caroline tugged on the sash of her robe. "Yes, it was quite a day."

Brenna smiled. "Joey was exhausted. He fell asleep in the bath."

"He needed a change, just as you said."

"Everyone—well, the staff, anyway—knows that you're behind all the things that have been happening lately. It's good of you to step in and help Delfina."

"I don't mind," Caroline said. "In fact, I rather enjoy it." In truth, it surprised Caroline that she did. This was a side of her that had awakened quite unexpectedly since arriving at Stephen's house.

"You're good at it, too," Brenna said. "Richard told me that Stephen has a very profitable deal in the works brought on, in part, by the wives of some businessmen coming over for tea and luncheon."

Pride swelled in Caroline. "I'm glad I could help."

"Of course, Delfina is getting all the credit."

"It's better that way," Caroline said. "I'm supposed to be working as a graphologist, not interfering with the running of the house.''

''That's generous of you.''

''Thank you,'' Caroline said. ''But that's not what you came to talk to me about, is it?''

Brenna studied her hands for a moment, then drew in a breath. ''I've decided to leave.''

''Leave? Leave here? Quit your job?''

''Yes,'' Brenna said, although saying it was clearly painful for her.

''But why?''

''I have to.''

''Don't you like it here?''

''Yes, of course.''

''Has Joey become too much for you?''

''Oh, no,'' Brenna said. ''Joey is a dear. A typical little boy, but a dear one.''

''Then what is it? Why are you leaving?''

Brenna squeezed her eyes shut for a moment. ''It's just so...difficult.''

''Richard, you mean.''

Brenna nodded miserably. ''And now he's going to the park with us on Sunday.''

''Don't you want him to go?''

''Of course I *want* him to. But—but it's so hard being around him when—''

''When you love him so much?''

Brenna let out a breath. ''Yes,'' she whispered. ''I love him and I'm poison for him.''

Caroline's heart ached along with Brenna's.

''He cares about you, too, Brenna. I see it in him

every time he looks at you, every time you're together.''

"But I'm all wrong for him. I'm—I'm not good enough for him. We both know it.'' Brenna pressed her fingers to her lips. "That's why I think it would be easier if I left.''

"There must be a way,'' Caroline said.

"There isn't. You know it, I know it, Richard knows it.'' Brenna sighed. "None of us will face it. And we must.''

"Leaving isn't the answer.''

"It might be,'' Brenna said. "If I'm not around, if Richard doesn't see me every day, he'll move on. He'll find himself a wife who can elevate him to the position he deserves.''

"You'd do that for Richard?'' Caroline asked. "You love him that much?''

Brenna pressed her lips together, holding back her tears. "I know how the world works. He'll never have anything if he marries me.''

"You don't know that for sure,'' Caroline said.

"Los Angeles, San Francisco, New York—the people are all the same. Richard will never be accepted if he's married to a woman of the working class.''

"But there're other places to live,'' Caroline offered.

"Richard knows people here, in this city. He can't start over someplace else.''

Brenna sank into the overstuffed chair, too weary to stand. Caroline sighed heavily, knowing Brenna was right, but not wanting to accept it. The upper class was an elite group. A tight, closed circle. She'd been accepted only because Delfina had introduced her and because her father was well-known in Europe. Brenna didn't have such an entrance.

"But what about Joey?" Caroline asked.

Brenna touched her finger to the corners of her eyes. "It will break my heart to leave him."

"He's already lost his mother, and not fully accepted it," Caroline said. "What will happen when you're gone? He'll have nightmares about losing you, too."

"I know. I've thought of that." Brenna looked at Caroline, her face drawn in deep lines. "But I just don't know what else to do."

"Something can be done," Caroline insisted. "I just have to think on it for a while."

"But we're going to the park on Sunday."

Caroline took Brenna's hand and pulled her to her feet. "Go and enjoy it."

"But—"

"It might be your only day with Richard," Caroline said. "You might have to leave, he might marry someone else. But you'll have that one day with him. Enjoy it. Enjoy each other."

"I don't know if I can do that," Brenna said. "It's so painful."

"Life hurts sometimes," Caroline agreed. "But wouldn't it be better to have one glorious day to remember than to have none at all?"

Brenna sniffled. "Yes, I suppose."

"Of course it would." Caroline gave her a hug. "Now, I'm going to do some thinking on your situation and see what I can come up with. And in the meantime, stop worrying. We'll go to the park on Sunday and have a fabulous time. All of us."

Brenna managed a weak smile. "I'm afraid to get my hopes up."

"Don't get your hopes up. Not yet, anyway. Just enjoy Richard and Joey on Sunday," Caroline said. "That's the best we can do right now."

Brenna pulled in a fortifying breath. "All right. I'll do it."

"Good."

Caroline walked with her to the door. Brenna turned back.

"What about you and Stephen?" she asked.

Caroline stopped still. "Stephen and me?"

"Yes," Brenna said. "There's something between the two of you. It's so obvious."

"You're just letting your own feelings for Richard spill over onto us," Caroline told her.

"No," Brenna said, shaking her head. "Look how you've become a part of his life so easily. Look at how you've taken over, all that you've done."

"That only means I'm a busybody who can't mind my own business," Caroline said.

"I've seen the way you look at him sometimes," Brenna said softly. "And the way he looks at you."

"You're mistaken," Caroline insisted. "Now, you get to bed and quit worrying about things. Joey will be up early and you'll need all your energy for him.''

Caroline eased Brenna out of her room and closed the door firmly behind her. What had Brenna been thinking? Suggesting something was going on between her and Stephen?

It wasn't like that, not at all. Caroline switched off the lamp at her bedside and slipped out of her robe. Just because she helped Delfina with the spring cleaning and redecorating the sitting room didn't mean anything significant. She'd done a few things to make Stephen's life easier and help him with his business. She shared the pride in Stephen's success, felt a joy in easing his burden, a satisfaction in joining in his work. But that didn't mean she was in love with him.

Love?

Caroline sank into the bed. True, he stirred a passion in her. He made her think very unladylike things—made her want to do very unladylike things. But what did passion have to do with marriage and a husband?

Caroline pulled the coverlet over her. In love? With Stephen?

How silly. She didn't even want a husband.

Did she?

Chapter Sixteen

When Stephen strode into the breakfast room the next morning, Caroline was surprised to see his jacket and vest unbuttoned and his collar open. She never saw him—except on the balcony—when he wasn't completely dressed, shiny, crisp and neat. She wasn't expecting this tiny intimacy between them.

He stopped across the table from her, reached into his pocket and pulled out two neckties.

"Which one?" he asked, and held them both up.

Caroline grinned. "Don't tell me you've lost your confidence."

"Just tired of being picked on," Stephen said, smiling. "Go ahead. Choose one, so I won't have to hear about it later today."

Caroline studied his navy pin-striped suit and the two neckties he held. "The maroon with the white stripe."

He frowned at his other selection, the gold-and-gray stripe. "What's wrong with this one?"

"It's ugly."

He looked offended. "I like it."

"Then I'll donate it to the church clothing drive with your kindest regards," Caroline said.

"That's what I get for asking," Stephen said, but didn't seem the least offended. He moved to the beveled mirror over the fireplace and looped the tie around his neck.

She'd never seen a man dress before. He lifted his chin to button his collar. His Adam's apple bobbed. With long, sturdy fingers he crossed the tie, pulled it snug against his throat.

"How long will it take you to complete those handwriting samples I gave you?" Stephen asked, looking at her in the mirror.

"Are you in a hurry for them?" Caroline asked.

He turned, closing up the buttons of his vest. "I'd like to have them by day after tomorrow."

"I can do that," she said.

"Good." Stephen buttoned his jacket and gave his necktie a final tweak. He spread his arms, offering himself for her inspection.

Caroline couldn't resist having him stand there an extra second or two. He was so handsome, and for these few moments he was all hers. She could look at him at her leisure, openly, brazenly, instead of catching quick peeks when she thought no one else noticed.

"Perfect," she declared.

He gave her a little bow. "Thank you."

Caroline held out her hand. "Give it here."

He winced. "You're sure?"

"Positive." She wiggled her fingers.

He huffed and laid the gold-and-gray necktie in her hand. "I still like it."

"Don't be hurt that your necktie selections are lacking," Caroline said. "There are still many things you do well."

Stephen sat down and paused as he reached for his napkin. "If only you knew."

Heat coiled in the pit of her stomach and surged through her. A flash of something else zinged along with it. It zapped Stephen, too. They exchanged a glance completely inappropriate for the breakfast table.

The maid came in then and served Stephen his breakfast, pouring coffee from the silver service on the buffet.

"Have you decided what to do about your Johannesburg situation?" Caroline asked, trying to finish her own breakfast without spilling something.

"Not yet," Stephen said. "Richard and I are still discussing it."

An awkward moment passed while Caroline tried desperately to think of something else to say. Without conversation, they were left to look at each other, and their looks were proving almost lethal. Of course, conversation didn't always help, either.

Finally, Caroline rose from the table. "I'll get to work now."

"Fine," Stephen mumbled.

He watched her leave, the gathers of her deep

purple dress swaying, tantalizing him, calling to him. The scent of her lingered in the room, and that didn't help anything.

He had to get her in bed. In that moment, Stephen knew it. There was no way around it. He'd tried to fight off his feelings for her—his lust for her. He could barely keep himself under control when he was around her. In fact, he could hardly contain himself when he simply thought of her.

Caroline Sommerfield was meant for moments between the sheets. Long, hot moments. Moments that stretched into hours, afternoons, nights—the days that followed.

Stephen ached for her. His body pulsed, throbbed. He wanted Caroline, plain and simple.

But actually getting her into his bed wouldn't be simple at all.

He toyed with his oatmeal and finally set his spoon aside. Caroline was a respectable, genteel woman. Even though she'd let him kiss her, and even kissed him back, she had to be treated carefully. He didn't want to scare her away.

He knew where her bedroom was. She'd even answered when he'd knocked on her French doors last night. How easy would it be to slip inside her room? Tonight?

Tonight was a long time off. His body couldn't wait that long. Maybe he could ask her to come up to his room now? Match up his neckties?

A trumped-up story to lure her away was an option. It had worked before, with an innocent invitation to see a new batch of kittens in the carriage house when he was fourteen. And worked well, too. Because when Mary Lynn Carmichael suggested it, he had gone along dumbly and spent thirty minutes in the loft with her that had changed his mind forever about the usefulness of girls.

Of course, to pull off a plan such as that took some finesse. At least it would with Caroline; he'd been an easy mark when Mary Lynn proposed it. But right now he wasn't thinking too clearly. He never did in this condition.

She was in his office now. Right now. Stephen's body warmed a few more degrees; his desire flamed hotter. His office. His desk. Caroline in her wide-brimmed hat and her high buttoned shoes. And nothing else.

Slumping forward, Stephen braced his elbows on the table and pressed his palms over his face. What the hell was he thinking? Caroline was a decent woman. He couldn't just barge into her bedroom, lure her upstairs to his room or have her naked on his desk.

Could he?

Stephen left the breakfast room.

He found Caroline seated at the little table in the corner of his office, working on the handwriting samples, head bent, lips pursed in concentration. Beautiful.

Too beautiful, arousing too urgent a need for any more thinking on Stephen's part.

He strolled into the office. "Caroline, could you

help me a moment? There're some kittens you might—"

"Kittens?"

"Neckties." Stephen pulled at his collar. "Neckties. They're neckties. I hoped you could help me match them up."

She looked pleased that he'd asked. "Really? You'd like my help?"

"Of course." He nodded casually toward the door. "They're upstairs."

"Upstairs?"

Stephen struggled to keep his face expressionless. "I could have all the suits and shirts and neckties brought down here, but heaven knows how long that would take. Aunt Delfi's got the servants off doing something. I never even see them anymore. But I could find them and have them cart it all down here, string it across the office—"

"No, that would be too much trouble," Caroline agreed.

He pressed his lips together to keep from smiling. "Then you'll come up and lend me your considerable talents?"

She looked around, unsure. Finally, she rose from the chair. "I suppose it would be all right. Just this once."

Just this once?

Caroline moved past him, trailing her delicate scent behind. A deep, profound ache caused him to shudder—a result of his need for her, rather than his conscience, or so he told himself.

Stephen watched her glide down the hallway toward the staircase, heading up to his bedroom, calling to him with each sway of her hips.

He wanted her. Right now, he wanted Caroline. He wanted her in his bed, on his desk, in the hallway—anywhere. He wanted to hold her, to be inside her, to own her. This minute. Just this once.

Stephen's lust for her warred with his conscience. Could he have her one time and walk away? Would that be enough to quench his desire for her?

Would he feel like a son of a bitch when it was over? Did she deserve that?

"Dammit…" Stephen mumbled under his breath, then went down the hallway after her. "Caroline?"

She turned. "Is something wrong?"

Once would never be enough. Not with Caroline. That realization was nearly as strong as his desire for her. She was intoxicating, but worse, she was addictive. Stephen would never get enough of her if he rolled around in bed with her for the rest of the week…the rest of his life.

He stopped in front of her and stood close, too close. She backed up a step. He followed. She bumped against the wall.

"Never mind about the neckties," Stephen said, and braced his arm against the wall, hating himself and his conscience for doing the decent thing.

"You're sure?"

Caroline gazed up at him with big, blue eyes. Their faces were inches apart, their bodies the same. Raw passion churned inside him.

"I'm...sure." The words hung in his throat for a moment, but he got them out.

"Another time?"

He wanted to press against her, feel her flesh give way to his. Wanted to kiss her, blend their mouths together.

Instead, Stephen stepped away. He would always want her this badly. It had become the one constant in his life.

Before, he'd believed differently. Nothing lasted a lifetime. Nothing was forever. In business he worked for today and built for tomorrow. With family—and women—he counted on neither.

Except maybe Caroline. Why was she different?

Stephen didn't know and he couldn't seem to think hard enough to come up with an answer. At least not at the moment.

He nodded down the hallway. "I've got work to do."

Stephen returned to his office, thick with need, aching with want.

What the hell was wrong with him? He fell into his chair. He'd used women once or twice and forgotten them. Thought nothing of it.

Why was it so different with Caroline? The only thing he knew for certain was that he couldn't bear to be with her and couldn't bear to be apart from her. And where did that leave him?

Caroline turned in a quick circle before the mirror in her dressing room. Yellow skirt, white-and-yellow striped blouse with a high collar, and a straw skimmer. She gave herself a nod of approval. Perfect for a Sunday afternoon at the park.

She gathered her small white handbag and parasol and left her room. Brenna and Joey were in the hallway just ahead of her. Joey, dressed in a white sailor suit, tugged at Brenna's arm, pulling her along behind him.

"Ready for the park, Joey?" Caroline asked, catching up with them.

He hopped up and down, nearly losing his hat. "They gots boats. Real boats. I can ride in them. Uncle Richard said so."

Brenna smiled down at the child. "He's been wound up like a top since he got up this morning."

"Good thing there's three of us to keep up with him." Caroline touched Brenna's arm. "Are you all right about going today?"

Brenna nodded. "I decided you're right. I'm just going to enjoy the day with Richard and not worry about tomorrow."

"Good," Caroline said. Brenna looked bright and happy in a pink dress and white hat, and Caroline was sure she meant what she said.

Richard waited at the bottom of the staircase, dressed casually in cream trousers and a brown checked jacket. His face lit up when he saw them.

Joey broke away from Brenna and rattled down the stairs.

"There's my boy," Richard said, and swung the child into his arms.

"Can we ride the boats first, Uncle Richard? Can we? I want to ride them all day!"

"We'll ride until we're sick," Richard promised. He turned to Caroline and Brenna. "And what a lucky man I am, to have two such beautiful women all to myself today."

"Not completely." Stephen came down the hallway wearing white trousers, a blue jacket and a straw boater. "I'd like to share in some of that good fortune," he said.

"I thought you were working today," Richard said.

"I decided a change of scenery might help," Stephen said. He looked at the women. "No objections, I hope?"

"Of course not," Brenna said. "It will be good for Joey to spend more time with you."

Caroline felt her stomach knot when Stephen turned to her. Having him along today wasn't something she'd planned on. But she decided to take her own advice to Brenna and just enjoy the day.

"The more the merrier," Caroline declared.

Joey wiggled out of Richard's arms and ran to the front door. "Let's go!"

The weather obliged with a warm, sunny afternoon as they climbed into the carriage. The picnic hamper Caroline had instructed Mrs. Branson to prepare was already in place, along with several throws and blankets. Caroline and Brenna sat on one seat, with Joey on the end and the men across from them.

"I invited Aunt Delfi to join us," Caroline said,

as the carriage pulled away, "but she already had plans."

"How much longer?" Joey asked, leaning against the window.

"Aunt Delfi's been doing so much better lately," Stephen said. "Not a single episode of dimming vision or numbing limbs."

"Why does it take so long?" Joey asked.

"I think she's finally come to terms with your uncle's death," Richard said.

"That's what I thought," Stephen agreed.

"I'm thirsty."

"What else could it be?" Stephen asked.

Caroline felt Brenna's gaze on her face, but didn't acknowledge her unspoken message. She didn't want to spoil the day by having Stephen remind her she was paid to be a graphologist and not his aunt's social secretary.

"How much longer?" Joey asked.

"Come here, little man." Richard wrestled the boy onto his lap. Brenna fished two miniature wooden horses from her handbag, toys that kept Joey occupied until they reached the park.

Westlake Park lay along Wilshire Boulevard on the outskirts of the city. Long an unsightly, overgrown ravine, the land was finally developed into a lake and park for recreation. Boating and afternoon concerts had recently been offered, making it a favorite spot for families.

As soon as the driver parked the carriage and opened the door, Joey shot out at a run.

"Joey!" Brenna shouted. "Stop!"

Richard scrambled out of the carriage ahead of her and caught the child before he'd gotten too far away. He led him back to the carriage by the hand and knelt down in front of him as the others climbed out.

"Miss Brenna is in charge," Richard told him. "You must listen to her and behave yourself, if you want to stay at the park."

Joey stomped his feet. "I want to ride the boats!"

"Then be good," Richard said sternly. "Don't run off. Stay with Miss Brenna. Understand?"

The little boy pouted for a minute, then nodded and latched on to Brenna's hand. "Can we see the boats now?"

She smiled. "Yes, by all means let's go see those boats."

With Joey between them, Richard and Brenna headed off toward the lake.

"I think you were right," Caroline said as she and Stephen followed. "Joey would have been a handful for Brenna and me today."

"And maybe you were right, too," Stephen said. "He needs to get out more often. It's hard, though. I like to keep him home where I know he's safe."

"Is that what your brother wanted?" Caroline asked. She wished the words back, afraid the memory would be hurtful for Stephen. But it didn't seem to be.

"I'm not sure. We never talked about it," Stephen said. "Tommy and Kellen were crazy about the boy. I don't want anything to happen to him."

"It's too bad Kellen left," Caroline said. "Joey still talks about them both."

Stephen gazed down at her. "He does? I thought he'd have forgotten by now."

"Brenna says he talks about his mama and papa a lot," Caroline said. "I suppose you never stop loving your parents, no matter what."

"If they're good parents," Stephen said. "Not all are."

Caroline sensed he was speaking of his own mother and father, but she didn't pursue the conversation. Stephen was already looking at the park, and the vacant land surrounding it.

"I wonder what this acreage is going for?" he mused.

Caroline tugged on his arm. "You're not supposed to be working today. Save your business dealings, your Johannesburg problem and your worries for tomorrow."

Stephen grunted noncommittally. "Oh, by the way, the Pinkerton agent caught our thief redhanded."

"Was it—"

"Rudy Acres, just as you said." He smiled down at her. "I guess I'm going to have to keep you around."

Caroline smiled but didn't say anything—couldn't have even if she'd wanted to.

The park was laid out with the lake and a large

red-roofed boathouse in the center. Tall trees offered shade. There were flowers and shrubs, and paths that wound through the grounds. Rowboats glided over the still water.

Vendors sold popcorn, caramel apples and cookies. There were lemonade stands. A goat hitched to a cart offered rides for the brave. Colorful balloons were for sale.

Young boys raced along the paths and climbed the trees. Girls played at the lake's edge, feeding the ducks. Picnickers were spread out on blankets under the shade trees. Couples sat on benches watching, listening, relaxing.

Joey took one look at the boats and decided he wanted no part of them. Brenna and Richard coaxed, but he refused to get in. So they all walked through the park together. Joey found some little boys his age and they became instant friends.

"You go ahead," Brenna said, sitting on a bench with a perfect view of the children. "I'll keep an eye on Joey."

"I could use a rest myself," Richard said, and sat down next to her.

Stephen offered his arm to Caroline. "Shall we?"

There was no reason not to, really, so she accepted and he led her toward the lake.

"Are you afraid of water?" Stephen asked.

"You're not going to toss me in, are you?" she asked.

He chuckled. "You'd just pull me in after you."

"Then what do you have in mind?"

"You'll see."

He took her to the boathouse and rented a rowboat for them. Caroline unfurled her white, lacy parasol against the afternoon sun and sat in the bow as Stephen rowed them across the lake.

"Are you glad you came?" Caroline asked.

"I am," Stephen declared. After all, he'd gotten to hold her hand assisting her into the little rowboat and now he had her all to himself. Not as good as having her in bed, but he'd take it.

"I've been trying to ask you something, and every time the subject comes up you avoid answering." Stephen stowed the oars, leaving them adrift in the center of the lake. "Now I have you to myself and you'll have to give me an answer."

They were in plain sight of a hundred people, with the lake the focal point of the park. Other boats skimmed the water nearby. Strollers followed the shore.

Yet alone with Stephen in the tiny boat, Caroline felt isolated, cut off from everyone and everything. It was just the two of them in their own little world.

"Since I seem to be at your mercy," Caroline said, "what is this burning question of yours?"

Stephen rested his arms on his drawn-up knees. "Why don't you want to get married?"

"That's a very personal question."

"I know. So answer it."

"For your information, Mr. Monterey, I've tried to answer that question every time you've posed it,"

Caroline said. "But whenever the subject comes up, you kiss me."

"I do?"

"You do."

"Well, don't get your hopes up this time—"

"My hopes up!"

"—because I'm not kissing you." He raised his eyebrows. "Until I get my answer, that is."

"Do you think you can just kiss me whenever you want?"

He wagged his finger at her. "You're changing the subject again."

"All right." Caroline straightened her skirt and gazed thoughtfully toward shore. "Well, let's see…"

"Are you just defying your father?" Stephen asked.

"No, that's not it."

"You've seen bad marriages that hurt people?"

Caroline shook her head. "No, not really."

"Is there some part of the…proceedings…you find distasteful?"

That was what he really wanted to know. Caroline didn't seem cold—not even cool. But if she had an aversion to the mere thought of sharing a bed with a husband, that was a different matter. Stephen wasn't sure why he wanted to know. Except that if he couldn't get her in bed with him, at least he could talk about it.

Caroline considered his question and knew exactly what he was getting at, what "proceedings" he referred to. She should have been shocked that he'd made such a suggestion to her. Shocked, outraged, horrified. She should insist he row her back to shore immediately, and go home in a huff.

Instead she looked at him directly. "Nothing about it seems distasteful. I used to live in France, if you'll recall."

His jaw sagged and he shifted on the wooden seat.

"The French are very progressive in their thinking on such matters," Caroline said softly. "A friend of mine had a book with diagrams that—"

"Stop." Stephen pulled his handkerchief from his pocket and mopped his brow. "You're getting off the subject again."

"I thought this *was* the subject."

"Just tell me why you don't want to get married," Stephen said, shoving the handkerchief into his pocket.

"This whole thing was my father's idea," Caroline said. "For some reason he got it into his head that I needed a husband. I'll never understand why."

"Something in you must have changed," Stephen said. "He recognized it and knew you were different, and were ready for a husband and family of your own."

Caroline spread her arms. "I don't feel any different."

"How old are you?"

"Goodness, but you're full of personal questions today," Caroline said. "I'm twenty-four."

"Old—not to be married. He should have sent you off to your aunt's for a husband years ago."

"I guess it didn't occur to him."

"Or he knew you weren't ready," Stephen said. "Until now."

"And why aren't you married?" Caroline asked.

"We're not here to talk about me." Stephen picked up the oars. "I'm hungry. Let's go."

"Not so fast." Caroline leaned forward and placed her hand on an oar. "I answered your question, now you answer mine."

"All right," Stephen said. "Nothing about it seems distasteful to me."

"That wasn't the question."

"I thought it was."

"No, that's just what you want to keep talking about," Caroline said. "Why haven't you married? Every mother, aunt and grandmother in the city considers you a prime catch."

Stephen grinned. "I'm good at dodging them. Lots of practice. Besides, I'm too busy working."

But Caroline thought it something different entirely. Work was easier for him to deal with because it involved nothing more than cold hard facts, business deals, a few personnel problems Stephen could keep at arm's length. There was nothing personal about it.

"I'm hungry," Stephen said again. He gave her a little smile and started rowing.

On shore once more they found Richard and Brenna seated at the same bench, with Joey playing under the trees with the little boys. Everyone agreed it was time to eat. Stephen wanted to know what Mrs. Branson had packed. They finally decided to picnic under the oaks overlooking the lake, then take in the afternoon concert at the bandstand. Richard set off to get the hamper from the carriage, and Stephen went to buy lemonade for everyone.

"That shady spot will be perfect," Brenna said. "We'll just—"

She turned in a circle, then whirled again.

"Oh, my God. Where's Joey?"

Chapter Seventeen

"Oh, my God. Joey!" Brenna turned, searched frantically. "Joey!"

"He can't have gone far," Caroline said. "Joey!"

Richard and Stephen came rushing back. Brenna pressed her hands to her lips. "Joey's gone."

Caroline turned to the trees. The little boys he'd played with were still there, their parents stretched out on blankets.

Strangers. People she didn't know. Caroline turned the other way. More strangers. Dozens of them. Everywhere.

She whirled. The lake.

Stephen caught her arm. "Caroline, you and Brenna check behind the trees and down the path toward the carriage. Richard, come with me."

The men set off toward the lake.

Brenna pressed her palms to her cheeks. "My God, Caroline, if something's happened to him—"

"Come on." Caroline pulled Brenna along with her.

She asked the parents of the little boys, but they hadn't noticed Joey wander away. They'd been busy eating, watching the boats on the lake, as well as keeping an eye on their own children.

Caroline and Brenna searched behind the trees and in the shrubs, calling Joey's name, then headed toward the path they'd used when they'd entered the park.

With a sick feeling, Caroline glanced at the lake. Joey hadn't been all that excited with the water. But what if he'd gotten up his nerve? What if he'd ventured too close? What if—

Caroline forced her thoughts to the task at hand. Conjuring up fantasies would serve no purpose. She and Brenna pressed on.

As the afternoon had worn on, the crowd had increased. More children had arrived, little boys wearing the popular, fashionable sailor suit that Joey wore. Caroline thought she spotted him twice.

"Caroline," Brenna said, "what if—"

"Keep looking," she said, refusing to think the worst.

They pushed through the crowd. Caroline glimpsed something white up ahead. A large man in a red-striped jacket stepped in front of her. She darted around him, rose on her toes, strained to see over the heads in front of her.

She spotted him again: a little boy in a sailor suit. A man held his hand as they walked away from her.

Caroline broke into a run, dodging people, holding up her skirt.

"Joey!"

The little boy looked back over his shoulder. It was him.

"Oh, Joey…" Caroline knelt in front of him, relieved, angry, thrilled. "Oh, Joey, we were so worried about you."

She looked up at the man who still held the boy's hand. He was nearly thirty, she guessed, dressed in work trousers, a wrinkled white shirt and brown vest. His face was lined, deeply tanned by the sun.

Caroline rose and took Joey's other hand. "Thank you for finding him," she said.

Brenna rushed up and lifted Joey into her arms. "Thank goodness, Joey, you're safe. Are you all right?"

Joey just shrugged, as if he didn't know what all the fuss was about.

"I'd better go find Richard and Stephen," Brenna said, and left.

"Bye, mister," Joey called, waving at the man who'd found him.

"Thank you again," Caroline said. "Where did you find him?"

He waved vaguely toward the lake. "Just wandering."

"I'm sure his uncle would like to meet you and give you a reward," Caroline said. "If you'll just—"

The man backed away. "I don't want anything."

A troublesome knot yanked in the pit of Caroline's stomach.

"Just forget it," the man said, and headed down the path.

Caroline watched, but lost him in the crowd. The knot in her stomach tightened.

When she caught up with Joey again, he was standing on a bench surrounded by Stephen, Richard and Brenna, all giving him a lecture about not wandering off, not talking to strangers, not doing as he was told.

Stephen looked so tall and sturdy, so capable. She wanted to fall into his arms and let him hold her up for a while.

Joey seemed relatively unconcerned, and when they were done, he jumped down and headed off to play with his friends again.

"It's my fault," Brenna said.

"It's all our faults," Richard said. "We were all there. All supposedly watching him."

"But I'm responsible," Brenna said. She looked up at Stephen. "I'm so sorry. If something had happened to him—"

"He's safe now. That's what matters," Stephen said.

But for Caroline, that wasn't the end of it.

"I think we could all use some lunch now," she said. "Stephen, will you help me with the hamper?"

"I'll get it. Wait here in the shade."

"No," she said. "I'll come with you."

They walked across the park and up the path to the carriage. Caroline found herself searching the faces of the people they passed, watching for the man who'd found Joey. She didn't see him, but her frazzled nerves didn't quiet down.

At the carriage, Stephen unloaded the hamper.

"I tried to get the man who found Joey to wait so you could meet him," Caroline said. "But he wouldn't. He left."

"Too bad." Stephen pulled blankets from the carriage and loaded them on top of the hamper.

Despite the fact that the incident had ended well, Caroline's heart still beat fast. She couldn't shake the eerie feeling that kept her spine tingling.

"Stephen…"

"What?" He lifted the hamper and blankets into his arms.

"Stephen, I—"

He gave her a second look, then dropped the whole lot again and slid an arm around her waist. "You're white as a ghost, Caroline—what's wrong?"

"Nothing…probably." Caroline gulped. "The man was just taking Joey around the park to find us, I'm sure. Hoping Joey could point us out. But…"

Stephen leaned closer. "What is it, Caroline? Tell me."

"When I saw them, Stephen, the man was leading Joey toward the carriages, away from the park."

Joey was sleeping soundly on Richard's shoulder when they arrived home. Everybody was worn out. Caroline was anxious to get into the bath and fall into bed.

Delfina waited in the sitting room off the foyer
when they came into the house. She met them
wringing her hands.

"Oh, dear, Stephen..." Delfina's worry lines
straightened as her eyes widened. *"Oh."*

"What's wrong, Aunt Delfi?" he asked.

"Joey..." Delfina gestured to the boy still in
Richard's arms. "He's *here.*"

"Of course he's here," Stephen said. "We took
him to the park, remember?"

"But..."

Caroline exchanged a troubled look with Stephen,
then slipped her hand around Delfina's elbow.

"Joey's been with us all day," Caroline said. "I
explained to you this morning that we were taking
him. I invited you to go with us. Remember?"

"Of *course* I remember," Delfi said. "But..."

"But what?" Stephen asked.

"Nothing," Delfina said quickly. She headed toward the rear of the house. "Caroline, *do* come,
won't you, dear?"

"Do you think she's all right?" Caroline whispered to Stephen.

He shrugged. "I've never known her to have any
mental lapse before, but she is getting older."

"I'd better see what she wants," Caroline said.
She followed Delfina down the hallway as the others
went upstairs.

If Delfina had suffered any confusion about
Joey's whereabouts today, none of it was evident
when Caroline met her in the parlor.

"I had the most *interesting* luncheon today," Delfina said, easing herself onto the settee. "Why didn't you tell me you were an expert at interpreting handwriting?"

"I thought you knew," Caroline said, taking the chair across from her.

"I knew you did *something* for Stephen," Delfina said. "You were the talk of the luncheon today."

"I was?"

"A graphologist. My *goodness*. How *exciting*. And to think I had to learn it from the other ladies. You're much too modest, Caroline." Delfina's lips pinched together and she lowered her voice. "Of course, I didn't tell them you were actually working here in that capacity. No, no, that would *never* do. The ladies still think you're my houseguest, which makes everything *perfectly* acceptable. I shudder to think what my brother Colin would have said. He was such a *stickler* for propriety."

Delfina went on. "Anyway, Virginia Cleary's daughter is in a bit of a quandary right now. She needs your help."

"What sort of help?" Caroline asked. She didn't know Virginia Cleary or her daughter.

"Virginia's daughter is in the enviable position of being courted by two men. Both fine, upstanding men, very well thought of."

"Virginia's mother must be thrilled," Caroline said, and thought of her aunt Eleanor.

"Well, of course," Delfina said. "But her daughter must choose one. That's why she needs your help.''

''She wants me to pick her husband?''

''Well, yes. By analyzing their handwriting.'' Delfina's face lit up in a bright smile.

Caroline shrank back in the chair. ''I couldn't possibly do that. I couldn't advise anyone on whom they should marry.''

''You don't have to *pick* one or the other,'' Delfina said. ''Simply give Virginia's daughter the *truths* hidden in her suitors' handwriting. You've done it at parties, I was told. That's what *Stephen* is having you do, isn't it?''

''Well, yes,'' Caroline admitted.

''Then why not do it for Virginia's daughter? You could help her avoid a grave mistake.''

The whole idea troubled Caroline. Offering advice. Choosing husbands. It was all so personal. When she'd learned her skill she never reckoned she'd become so involved with the intimate details of other lives.

And it was merely her opinion. She would be shaping other people's futures based on her opinion of their handwriting.

She'd worried the same way after she'd named Rudy Acres as the thief at Stephen's warehouse and he'd turned the case over to Pinkerton. She'd caused a man to be sent to jail.

Stephen's words echoed in her mind. She'd done the right thing, and no one should feel bad for doing the right thing.

This was what graphology was intended for. She'd acquired the knowledge, learned the craft and was now obligated to share it. If it helped, if it kept Virginia Cleary's daughter from marrying a bad seed, then it would serve a good purpose. Caroline would be doing an injustice if she refused to help.

And this was the job she wanted for the rest of her life. Wasn't it?

She rose from the chair. "Tell Virginia Cleary I'll be happy to look at the handwriting of her daughter's prospective suitors."

"Excellent. Virginia will be so *pleased.*"

Caroline left the parlor thinking Delfina was the most pleased.

Over the next several days Caroline thought she'd go cross-eyed looking at handwriting samples. She finished up the batch Stephen's business associates had passed her way, only to have more appear on her desk. It seemed Stephen was singing her praises to everyone he knew.

It pleased Caroline that he thought so much of her work. She spent hours writing detailed reports on each sample—each person—then moving on to the next. Several of the businessmen she did work for wrote her letters of appreciation and recommendation. Stephen kept a copy of each of them tucked inside a folder in his desk drawer—for her personnel file, he said.

When she wasn't working on the samples Stephen gave her, Delfina kept her busy with more of the same. Virginia Cleary's daughter's suitor problem was handled easily enough, but once word got out, more mothers brought samples for Caroline to interpret.

Avoid relationships with those men whose *t*-bar is missing, she advised, and those with hooks on capital letters. Be wary of a strong diagonal starting stroke for any letter, or a *g* with a plain, straight stem. The list of unfavorable handwriting traits went on and on.

As did the favorable traits. A slight right slant was a good sign, along with rising lines, *y*'s with a very full loop, and small, round *i* dots.

It still bothered Caroline that she was affecting the outcome of the lives of other people. Stephen seemed to sense that and encouraged her to keep going. He didn't even mind that she worked on the samples of Delfina's friends at her little table in his office.

Of course, that left her with little time free to organize teas and luncheons for Delfina. The spring cleaning had been completed to her satisfaction and the pink sitting room was almost finished. Caroline kept a notepad beside her and jotted down things in the house that needed her attention. The list grew and grew until she found herself devoting as much time to it as the handwriting analysis.

"Here are more samples," Stephen said, dropping an envelope on her work table.

She looked up. "More?"

The late afternoon sun was obscured somewhat

by a layer of clouds outside, but a smattering of light managed to brighten Stephen's office. She'd been working since early morning and was just finishing up for the day—or so she thought.

"Yes," Stephen said. "I'd like you to get those done as quickly as possible. I've something more important for you to handle."

Glumly, Caroline pulled the stack of samples from the envelope. Some days—like today—when she sat at her little table, peering at ink strokes through her magnifying glass, she wished she could be with Delfina instead, preparing for a luncheon, organizing the staff or decorating another room in the big house. Her chosen profession was proving a bit confining.

"Well, all right," Caroline said, trying to muster some enthusiasm.

"Don't you want to know what the more important project is?" Stephen asked.

"Of course," she said, hoping she sounded interested.

"I've decided what to do about my Johannesburg problem," Stephen stated.

Caroline brightened. This was more interesting than what she'd spent her day working on.

"I'm replacing Clayton Girard," Stephen said. "He's no longer in charge of the operation there."

"Are you sure that's what you want?"

He nodded. "I'm sure. Richard and I discussed it at length. Richard knows the area as well as I—

probably better—and we agreed it's for the best. Girard will be gone as soon as I find a replacement.''

Caroline's heart sank a little. ''I guess you'd like me to analyze the handwriting of prospective replacements?''

''Of course.'' Stephen smiled down at her. ''All the other businessmen I've referred to you are very pleased with what you've done, Caroline. You're responsible for hiring nearly a dozen new employees for four different companies. You should be proud.''

''Yes, I suppose I should.''

Stephen tapped the samples on her desk. ''Better get busy. I'll be interviewing for the Johannesburg position tomorrow and I'll want your analysis right away.''

Caroline sighed heavily. ''All right. I'll get right on it.''

At that moment Delfina steamed into the office.

''Stephen, dear, I *must* have Caroline immediately,'' she announced.

Delfina didn't wait for his answer, just marched directly to Caroline's worktable and stood there until she got up. Caroline didn't waste a minute. She hurried out with Delfina, not even looking at Stephen.

''You must *see* this,'' Delfina said.

She led the way to the pink sitting room, which was, in fact, now pink.

Delfina gestured grandly into the room. ''Isn't it lovely? The workmen just left. Isn't it perfect?''

The room still smelled of paint and wallpaper paste when Caroline stepped inside. The ceiling now

boasted a scene of pinkish cherubs on a pale blue
background frolicking among white, puffy clouds.
The new tile floor gleamed. Drapes, furniture, rugs,
paintings were scheduled for delivery later in the
week.

"Just as we imagined," Caroline said. "Are you
happy?"

"Thrilled," Delfina said. "Which is the reason I
wanted to talk with you, Caroline. Something very
important *just* occurred to me as I was watching the
workmen leave."

"What's that, Aunt Delfi?"

"Since your arrival I've noticed how much more
efficiently the house has run. You've taken over everything so well, Caroline. The staff, the cleaning,
the menus. And you've organized so many wonderful events to enhance the Monterey name in the
community. It's all so *grand*."

Caroline smiled, glad to hear Delfina's first words
of gratitude for all she'd done in the Monterey
home.

"So," Delfina said, "I've decided this must be
made a permanent arrangement."

Caroline's heart began to beat a little faster. "Permanent? How?"

Delfina drew in a deep breath. "I've decided Stephen should get married."

"M—married?"

"Yes. And you, Caroline, will help pick out his
wife."

Chapter Eighteen

Caroline slept late, then languished in the big tub in her bathroom for nearly an hour. Delfina had provided a maid for her, but Caroline shooed her away after she'd helped with her hair, and now sat staring at her reflection in the mirror above her vanity table.

Stephen. Getting married.

And what was worse, she had to help select his wife.

Of all the times for Delfina to come up with an idea of her own. Absently, Caroline picked up a silver hand mirror and gazed at herself more closely. Oh, it was a good idea, all right. A poetry contest sponsored by the Monterey family, with the prize a donation to the orphanage in the winner's name.

Except that, actually, Stephen was the prize.

Using the poems, Delfina intended to have Caroline analyze the handwriting and select the best wife. What a perfect plan. Delfina had been beside herself with excitement. Caroline had sunk to despair.

She laid the mirror aside and rose from the satin-covered stool. Why did it bother her so much? Why did she care if Stephen married?

She'd enjoyed her day at the park with him so much. He'd been relaxed, actually talking about something other than business, which consumed most of his thoughts. Caroline doubted he would ever run barefoot through the backyard and dip his toe in the fountain as she'd suggested that night on the balcony, but he'd loosened up that day in the park. He'd made her laugh.

And he'd looked so confident and in charge when Joey had gotten lost. Stephen was a strong man. He didn't wait for anyone else to make decisions. She liked that about him.

Caroline sat on the edge of her bed and stared at her toes. There were lots of things she liked about Stephen. The way he looked in his undershirt. The way he kissed her. The way he made her feel about herself.

But how could that be? Caroline sprang off the bed. Why would she even think such things about Stephen? Or about any man, for that matter?

She didn't want a husband. She didn't want marriage. Her sole reason for agreeing to come to Los Angeles was to work for the Pinkerton Detective Agency, despite what her father and aunt had planned for her. Marriage was too confining. Staying in one house forever, overseeing its mundane chores. Never going anyplace new, or seeing anything different.

What had changed? Somehow, she'd involved herself in every aspect of the Monterey household—and found she loved it.

Caroline paced the floor, her footsteps silent on the floral carpet. When had she changed? When had it happened?

She stopped then and thought again of the afternoon in the rowboat with Stephen. He'd suggested that her father had seen a change in her and had sent her off to find a husband. Could that be right? Had she changed and not realized it?

At the moment, Caroline wished her father were there for her to talk to, confide in, take comfort from. Aunt Eleanor and Sophie had been to the Monterey home for tea, but Caroline didn't feel close to them. They were family, but strangers just the same.

Caroline pressed her hand to her lips, fighting back the tears that burned her eyes. If that were true, then what she'd felt all along, what she'd tried to ignore, was the simple fact that she'd fallen in love. With Stephen Monterey.

It was nearly noon when Caroline went downstairs. The lights were burning because of the cloudy sky, which matched her mood. She'd dressed the part, as well, in a gray shirtwaist with white lace collar and cuffs; she'd wished for black instead.

The ache she carried in her chest had now been identified as her love for Stephen. She'd cried over it and finally pulled herself together with the realization that just because Delfina wanted Stephen to marry, that didn't mean Stephen would grant his aunt's wish. Poetry contest winner or not.

At any rate, Caroline had to discuss it with him. She had to know how he felt about marriage...about her. Even though she wasn't feeling particularly reasonable at the moment, it was the reasonable thing to do.

Stephen's nose was deep in a ledger when she walked into his office. Thankfully, Richard wasn't there.

"Congratulations," Caroline said.

He glanced up. "On what?"

"You're getting married."

"Oh, that." Stephen turned back to his ledger.

Caroline stopped at his desk. "You know about it?"

"Aunt Delfi informed me this morning." He opened another ledger, flipped through the pages and compared figures to the ledger already opened.

"And that's all right with you?" she asked, feeling herself start to tremble.

"Actually," he said, without looking up, "I've thought about getting married for a while now."

"You *have?*" Caroline almost shouted the words at him.

Stephen grunted an answer, then pulled a set of documents from a stack on the corner of his desk. "Look these over, will you?"

She took the papers from him. "Did your aunt tell you about the poetry contest?"

He wagged his finger at the documents. "These are important. I want to know if both were written by the same person."

"Stephen, did you hear what I said?" Caroline asked. "Your aunt intends to—"

"The documents, Caroline. Now."

His frown deepened and she realized he was in no mood to listen to her. Well, she wasn't in the best of moods, either.

Caroline planted her hands on her hips. "Don't order me around!"

His expression hardened for a half second, then softened marginally. "Caroline, would you please look at those documents? I want to know if they are both—"

"—written by the same person. Yes, I know. You told me." Caroline stomped over to her little table and sat down.

She was being unreasonable and knew it, but under the circumstances, she felt entitled. She'd just realized that for the very first time in her life she was in love. In love with *him.* And she couldn't even tell him because his aunt intended to marry him off to someone else, and that seemed to be all right with him.

Thunder rumbled outside. Caroline forced herself to concentrate on the two documents she'd just been handed. She was too upset to discuss it rationally with Stephen. She'd be better off keeping her mind on her job for now, gathering her thoughts, then discussing it later.

That proved easier than she'd imagined. Caroline read the documents over. One was a personal letter, dated twenty-two years ago, from a George Monterey to Colin Monterey. The other was a business contract, dated twenty years ago.

The personal letter was just that, personal. News of the family, business, the weather.

The contract was for a piece of property promised by George Monterey to another man in exchange for farming the land for twenty years. That other man was Russell Pickette.

Caroline laid her magnifying glass aside. Pickette was the farmer whose family Stephen had left in their wagon during the heat of the afternoon with no refreshments. The farmer who'd made Stephen so angry. The farmer he'd refused to discuss.

Caroline rose from her chair. "Who is George Monterey?"

Stephen's gaze came up quickly. "Don't concern yourself with the details. Just write up your report."

"Is he another uncle? A cousin?" She approached his desk. "Your father?"

He flinched, and Caroline knew she had her answer.

"He's your father, isn't he?"

"Yes," Stephen replied tightly.

"And Russell Pickette is the farmer who was here to see you that afternoon."

Deep, intense anger stirred in Stephen. Caroline saw it in the quick tic of his jaw, the narrowing of his eyes.

She held out the documents. "Your father gave Mr. Pickette a two-hundred-acre parcel of land?"

"No. That document is a forgery."

"You told me Mr. Pickette was no one. When I asked, you said to forget about him, he didn't matter." Caroline thrust the documents at Stephen. "But he does matter!"

Stephen rose to his feet. "That isn't your concern. Just analyze the damned contract and give me your answer. That's what you're here for! Do your job!"

Breath left Caroline in a horrified rush. She stared up at him, trying to make sense of what he'd just said, what it meant. Then it came to her and she wished she hadn't figured it out at all.

"That's why you hired me," she said softly. "This document…this was the reason all along."

"It's a forgery! My father would never have agreed to give that land to Pickette. I needed you to prove it. What's wrong with that?"

"It's deceitful! You gave me this job for your own personal gain. You allowed me to believe you thought my work was of some value. You led me on." Caroline's chest ached as the full impact of what he'd done hit her. "That's why you referred me to those other businesses. I'm not stupid, Stephen. I can see that this contract will end up in court. You did all of this so I'd testify your way."

"My father didn't give that land to that stupid, ignorant farmer. He wouldn't do that." Stephen pounded his fist on the desk. "I refuse to believe that! And I won't let that Pickette bastard make a fool out of me!''

"What has any of this got to do with *you?*"

"It has everything to do with me!"

"Mr. Pickette has lived on that land for twenty years," Caroline said. "He has a wife. They've raised their children there. It's their home, Stephen."

"I don't give a damn about their home and their children," Stephen said. "You don't understand."

"Then explain it to me!"

"My father…" Color drained from Stephen's face. He touched his hand to his chest. "My father—"

"What, Stephen? What did he do?"

He backed away. From her, from what he'd started to say.

"It doesn't matter about him," Stephen said. "He's not your concern."

"You can't tell me, can you?" Caroline said. "You can't get the words out. You're so used to hiding behind your desk, your work, and covering up your feelings you can't even tell me what's wrong."

"I'm not hiding behind anything," Stephen told her. "I just want you to tell me that contract is a fraud. That's all!"

Caroline drew herself up. "I'm not going to tell you anything. You've just been using me. You pretended to appreciate my work, when you were really just building my reputation for your own good. And all your talk about my not feeling responsible for Rudy Acres—that was just so I'd keep working, wasn't it? It was all a big lie!''

''Dammit, Caroline—''

She slapped the documents down on his desk and ran out of the room.

''Caroline!''

She heard a crash inside his office. Caroline kept running, out the front door and down the street. She climbed onto the trolley car at the corner as raindrops fell and mingled with her tears.

''Stephen? Stephen, dear?''

He didn't turn away from the window when his aunt came into his office. Fat raindrops spattered against the panes, the flowers, the brick walkways in the rear lawn. Stephen leaned his forehead against the cool glass, staring out.

''Have you see Caroline?'' Delfina asked.

Stephen turned then, his shoulders hunched, hands thrust deep in his pockets, but didn't meet his aunt's eyes.

''She's gone,'' he said, the words slipping through his lips with some effort.

Delfina skirted around the pile of ledger books Stephen had heaved to the floor in a fit of anger. ''When will she be back?''

''She's...she's not coming back.''

''*What?*''

Stephen dropped into his chair. He was tired. Everything ached—his head, his chest. His heart?

"But she can't be *gone*," Delfina cried.

Rubbing his palms over his face, Stephen looked up at her. "She is."

"You can't let her leave, Stephen. You *can't*."

He rubbed his neck. "It was her choice."

"But you *must* bring her back, Stephen, you *must*. *Who* is going to plan the menus and oversee the staff? Who will direct the workmen to finish the sitting room? And what about the Monterey name? Who is going to plan our functions?"

He dismissed her concern with a brush of his hand. "You'll just keep at it, Aunt Delfi. You're doing an excellent job."

"Me?" Delfina waved her arms frantically. "I didn't do those things. *Caroline* did."

He looked up at her. "Caroline did all that?"

"Of *course* she did. Who *else* would have?"

Stephen mumbled a curse under his breath, directed at himself, and went back to the window. Behind him Aunt Delfi continued to fret, but he didn't listen. Caroline filled his mind.

She'd done all those things? She'd taken over his house, helped his aunt, planned the family's events? And he hadn't even realized it?

How easily Caroline Sommerfield had blended into his life. He could see that now, but before he'd wanted nothing more than to get her into his bed. That first night, he'd wanted her on his desk in her wide-brimmed hat and high buttoned shoes.

And all along she was winding her way into his home, his life, his heart. Even then, when he was panting after her, wondering about those French books with the diagrams she'd mentioned at the park, something else had tugged at him, something that went beyond lust. He hadn't known what it was.

Stephen knew now.

But now was too late. Caroline was gone.

Stephen awoke with a start. His eyes searched the darkened room. Faint light shone from the hallway. Where was he?

Outside the wind howled. He sat up, his body aching and sore, and realized he'd fallen asleep at his desk in his office.

Something was wrong. Stephen shook his head, trying to clear his thoughts. The sleep that had eluded him until long into the night held him in a tight grip now, refusing to let go.

Raindrops beat against the glass panes. The wind screamed around the windows. Screamed like he'd never hear it before.

Stephen shot to his feet, tipping his chair over. The screaming wasn't from the wind.

In the dark he ran out of his office, down the hallway, took the steps two at a time. The screams grew louder. His heart pounded.

On the second floor, Stephen slid to a stop. Light streamed out of the nursery. Brenna, wearing her nightgown, stood in the hallway, clutching a piece of paper in her hand and screaming.

He pounded on the door with his fists, rivaling the thunder in the night sky. He kicked the wooden panels, shook the knob until he thought it would come off in his hand.

"Open the door!" Stephen bellowed. "Open the damned door!"

The key clicked in the lock. Stephen barreled through.

"Where is she?" he demanded. "Where's Caroline?"

Aunt Eleanor, huddled in her flannel robe, cowered. "Really, Mr. Monterey, I must insist—"

Stephen darted through the house to the staircase and charged up the steps.

"Caroline!"

He screamed her name and went from room to room, forcing the doors open, peering into the darkness. He found her near the end of the hall.

"Caroline."

She roused from under the covers and pushed her hair away from her face.

"Stephen? What on earth—"

He caught her hand and pulled her from under the tangle of bedcovers. "You have to come with me. Now, Caroline."

No jacket or hat had protected him from the weather. Rain had soaked his shirt, his hair, his face.

"What's happened?" she asked.

"Joey," he said. "He's been kidnapped."

Chapter Nineteen

Rain fell as the carriage pulled to a stop in front of the Monterey home, the only house on the block with all its lights on at this predawn hour.

Caroline wore her aunt's cape over the same gray shirtwaist she'd had on when she'd arrived at Eleanor's house earlier, wiping away tears; she'd refused to answer her aunt's questions and had gone straight up to her old room.

Charles, impeccably dressed even at this hour, took her cape in the vestibule. Several men in suits walked purposefully through the foyer, one jotting down notes.

"The Pinkerton Agency," Stephen explained, as he took her hand and led her up the stairs. His clothing was soaked through but he didn't seem to notice.

Caroline lifted her skirts, hurrying to keep up with him. "Did you notify the authorities as well?"

"They're here. Somewhere."

When they reached the nursery more men were

there checking things, making notes, murmuring among themselves. Brenna was on the window seat, crying. Richard was beside her.

Caroline went to her, hugged her, and that brought on a new wave of tears.

"I'm so glad you're here," Caroline said to Richard.

He kept an arm securely around Brenna. "Delfina telephoned me. I came right over."

"It's—it's all my fault." Brenna sobbed into her hands.

"No, it's not," Richard said softly, stroking her hair.

"It is!" Brenna insisted. She looked up at Stephen with tears rolling down her cheeks. "I'm so sorry.... I woke up and he was—gone. Just gone..."

Brenna collapsed into tears again.

"It's not your fault," Richard told her again, more forcefully this time. He looked up at Stephen. "Tell her. Tell her it's not her fault."

Stephen didn't. Anger, frustration seethed in him.

"It's not her fault." Richard surged to his feet. "Tell her!"

"It is her fault! It's my fault! It's everybody's fault!" Stephen dragged his hand across his mouth, his anger dissipating. "It's nobody's fault."

Caroline rose and held Stephen's arm. "Brenna is hysterical. She needs to lie down. You should send for the doctor. And change your clothes, Stephen, you're soaked."

He nodded and looked relieved at having something to do.

"I'll stay with Brenna," Caroline said.

"No," Richard said. "I'll take care of her."

He lifted her in his arms and carried her to her bedroom, which adjoined the nursery. Caroline went with them. She tucked Brenna under the covers.

"I'll send the doctor up as soon as he arrives," she said.

But Richard didn't seem to hear. Caroline left him seated at Brenna's bedside, holding her hand, stroking her hair.

Caroline went to Delfina's room, sure the doctor would have to pay a call on her, too. Instead she found Delfina stretched out on the chaise, sipping tea, staring out at the first rays of dawn breaking through the cloud cover.

"Are you all right?" Caroline pulled over a footstool and sat at Delfina's side.

"Yes," she replied. "I am."

"I've sent for the doctor," Caroline said. "Brenna has fallen to pieces."

"I should have thought of that myself," Delfina said. She patted Caroline's hand. "Go to Stephen. He'll need you."

"You're sure you're all right?"

"Of course, dear," Delfina said, and turned back to the window.

Caroline found Stephen in his office. He'd changed out of his wet clothes and now wore navy trousers held up by suspenders, and a plain white shirt opened at the collar. He paced behind his desk.

A deep anxiety hung in the room, in the whole house. It permeated everything and everyone in it.

"I telephoned the doctor," Stephen said. "He's on his way."

Caroline went to the liquor cabinet in the corner of the office and took out a glass and a bottle of bourbon.

Stephen shook his head. "I don't drink, usually."

"This isn't for you," Caroline said. "It's for me."

She poured herself a shot. Stephen walked over and got another glass.

"What the hell…" He held it out to her.

Caroline filled his glass and they both tossed them back. Heat scorched her chest and tears sprang to her eyes.

"That's better," she wheezed, and set her glass aside. "Now, tell me what happened."

"I'd fallen asleep here at my desk," Stephen said. "I woke to Brenna's screaming. She'd gotten up to check on Joey and he was gone."

"You called the police? And the Pinkerton people?"

Stephen started pacing. "They found some mud and wet footprints in the kitchen. That's probably how the kidnappers got into the house."

"What about in the hallway and on the steps?"

"No, just in the kitchen. The detective theorized

they hadn't counted on the rain, so they took off their shoes after they entered the house.''

"Considerate of them," Caroline mumbled. "How did they know where the nursery was?"

Stephen shrugged. "It wouldn't be hard to figure out if they'd watched the house for a while."

"Any idea who's behind this?"

"Lots of ideas, unfortunately." Stephen touched his neck. "I went over all of this with the detectives. A business rival. Or a guest at my birthday party who had access to the house."

Caroline gasped. "The workmen. Oh, Stephen, I had those workmen in here for the sitting room. They were all over the house."

"Then there's always the servants. The detectives asked about a disgruntled employee."

"Rudy Acres…"

"Possibly," Stephen said. "There's the issue with Girard in Johannesburg. I'd begun interviewing for his position. Girard has friends here. They might have gotten word somehow."

Caroline slumped into the chair in front of Stephen's desk. "So many possibilities."

"When I find the villain responsible for this…" Stephen slammed his fist into his palm.

She went around his desk and touched his arm. He was tight with anger. "Yes, I know. But right now we have to think, Stephen."

With some effort, he calmed. "The detectives are interviewing the staff."

"What did the note say?" Caroline asked. "There was a ransom note, wasn't there?"

"It just said I'd be contacted later and that Joey was safe."

"Let me see it," Caroline said.

Stephen waved away her remark and turned to gaze out the window. "That's all it said. No more details."

"Don't you want me to look at the handwriting? Isn't that why you brought me here?"

He whirled around, staring at her blankly. "No...I hadn't even thought..."

Stephen took a step closer. "I didn't bring you here tonight because I wanted a graphologist," he said softly. "I just wanted *you,* Caroline."

She thought her legs would give out. Caroline braced her arm against the desk to hold herself up. She wanted to run to him, throw herself in his arms, but didn't have the opportunity.

Stephen turned back to the window. The last of the rain misted against the panes as the clouds on the distant horizon broke up. He was silent for a long while.

"You were right," he said, and the words sounded as if they hurt. "I hired you just for that one document, the land contract between my father and Pickette. I needed you to be a credible witness, so I got other businessmen to use your services. It was business, just business. But somehow it turned...personal."

Caroline's arms ached with the need to hold him.

But he kept himself just far enough away that she couldn't touch him.

He looked back at her. "I'm sorry. And I meant what I said about Rudy Acres. You did the right thing and have nothing to feel bad about. You're very good at your work. I'm...very sorry."

Turning back to the window, Stephen stared out again. All Caroline could do was stand near him and see the tight lines of his profile as he spoke, while her heart ached for him.

"My father—" Stephen cleared his throat and tried again. "My father inherited the same amount of money as did his brothers. You can see what my uncle Colin did with his inheritance. The other brothers did equally well. All except for my father.

"He was no businessman. Not by any stretch of the imagination. Only he didn't know he wasn't a businessman. He lost every cent—slowly, stupidly—with one bad deal after another. Ridiculous, idiotic schemes that no one with a grain of sense would look twice at. And, in the process, he became the laughingstock of the Monterey family and the business community."

Stephen turned to her then. "The joke of the business world was my father. I was his son, raised in his shadow. Do you know what that was like? How humiliating it was? Being laughed at, made fun of by people who matter? Always just a little on the outside, never quite as good as everyone else?"

"It must have been difficult for you," Caroline

said quietly, and she could see by his face that it had been.

"I couldn't afford to make a mistake. I'd be compared to my father—laughed at, just as he was. My uncle had taken me in, showed some faith in me. I couldn't let him down. I couldn't be anything less than…"

"Perfect."

Stephen turned away sharply. "I have a business deal—a very large deal—in the works right now for that property Pickette has been farming. His twenty-year lease is up this month. Then, from out of nowhere, he showed up on my doorstep waving that contract, claiming my father had made that agreement with him."

"And you thought you'd distanced yourself from all that," Caroline said. "But your father came back to haunt you one last time."

"He wouldn't have done that," Stephen said grimly. "My father was a bad businessman, but he would never have agreed to give that prime piece of real estate to the farmer who'd been nothing but a caretaker. He wouldn't have!"

Anger and hurt rolled through Stephen. She saw it in the tightness of his shoulders, the clenching of his fists. Tears welled in Caroline's eyes. How she wanted to hold him. Comfort him. Take away all his pain and make him better.

"My uncle is gone," Stephen said hoarsely. "My little brother. Now Joey—all I have left—is gone, too."

"Oh, Stephen…"

Caroline couldn't bear it another second. She went to him, tried to embrace him, but Stephen shrugged away from her. He strode out of the room.

She cried anyway, without him, for him. All of Stephen's troubles were now hers. All his pain, too. She cried for the little boy who'd tried so hard to be perfect, who'd grown into the man still striving for the same unattainable goal. She cried for herself because she loved him so much, and for Joey, and Brenna and Richard. For everyone in the Monterey home she'd come to love.

When her tears finally stopped, Caroline washed her face, blew her nose and searched out the Pinkerton detectives. They spared her only one indulgent moment, but that was enough, all she needed. Caroline went to the attic, then to Delfina's room.

"Why?" she asked, standing over the older woman still stretched out in her chaise. Caroline held up the ransom note the Pinkerton detective had reluctantly let her have.

"Why?" Caroline asked again.

Delfina set her teacup aside calmly. "That *brother* of mine. Colin. *Always* insisting on perfection. Everything had to be just *so*. How could *any* of us live up to his standards?"

Caroline waved the ransom note. "But how could you have gone along with this?"

Delfina turned her attention out the window again. "Some decisions are easily made."

Caroline went to her room and tucked all the cash

she'd accumulated in her underwear drawer into her handbag. She pinned her hat on and shrugged into a black cape.

The house had seven entrances. She slipped quietly out through the solarium and down the walkway to West Adams Boulevard.

A fine mist blew as she boarded the trolley and paid her nickel fare. At Second Street and Santa Fe Avenue she went inside the La Grande Station and bought her ticket. She waited for nearly an hour for the train.

Unaware the whole time that she was being followed.

Chapter Twenty

The train pulled into the station at Redlands nearly three hours later, after stops in Rancho Cucamonga and San Bernardino. Caroline hadn't moved from her seat. The train was crowded and she didn't want to give up her view out the window.

She'd never seen orange trees before. Hundreds of the trees, which looked more like big green bushes, spread out across the valley and over the foothills. The imposing San Bernardino Mountains loomed over everything.

The ticket agent in the Redlands station gave her directions to the address she inquired about, and since it wasn't far, she set out on foot.

The rain and clouds had been left behind in Los Angeles. Here in this quaint little town, the sun shone and a mild breeze blew. None of which lifted Caroline's spirits.

A mixture of houses lined the streets—grand homes with wide, sweeping porches and beveled windows, and smaller homes, modest but clean and well tended.

Caroline pulled from her handbag the envelope that she'd brought from the attic in the Monterey home, and verified the address one last time. Across the street was a white, two-story home with blue shutters and window boxes, the house she sought. Caroline said a quick prayer, crossed the street and knocked on the door.

It was quiet inside the house. The drapes were drawn in the front windows. She knocked again.

Presently, the door opened and a man looked out at her. He was thirtyish, with brown hair and a deeply tanned face.

The man at the park.

Caroline gasped. He recognized her at the same stunned moment and tried to push the door closed.

"No, wait, please." She braced her arm against it. "I just came to make sure he's all right."

"I don't know what you're talking about, lady. Now, get on out of here."

"No, please," Caroline said. "I've come alone. No one knows I'm here. I won't cause any trouble. I swear."

Someone spoke from inside the house. Caroline couldn't hear the words, but the man opened the door and waved her inside.

A woman about her age stood in the neat little parlor. Dark haired, pretty, a little too thin, she looked drawn and tired.

"Kellen?" Caroline asked.

Her shoulders sagged and she crossed her arms across her stomach. "Yes," she said. "I'm Kellen. And you're Caroline Sommerfield. Aunt Delfi told me about you."

"The whole family is worried sick about Joey."

"Yes, I know. And I'm sorry. Really I am," Kellen said. "But I had to have my baby back."

"He's here, then," Caroline said. "You do have him."

Kellen smiled faintly. "He's here. Sleeping like an angel. This is my brother, Lyle O'Hara."

"You tried to take him that day in the park, didn't you?" Caroline asked.

Lyle nodded. "Tried to."

"How did you know we'd be there?" Caroline asked.

Kellen sighed slowly and looked at her brother. He nodded.

"I guess I have no choice," Kellen said. She waved toward the back of the house. "We were about to have some coffee. Please sit down. I'll tell you what you want to know."

"You women need to hash this out," Lyle said, and took his hat from the peg beside the door. "I'll head on down to the market and get what we need for supper."

Kellen led the way down the short hallway to the kitchen at the back of the house. The cupboards and tile floor were neat and well scrubbed. Tall windows let in the sunlight and the view of the large backyard.

"The house belongs to Lyle," Kellen said, getting cups from the cupboard. "He has orange groves outside of town that are doing very well."

"I heard you'd moved to your mother's in Georgia," Caroline said.

Kellen managed a small smile. "I imagine you've heard a lot of things about me."

"Not really." Caroline unpinned her hat and draped her cape across one of the ladder-back chairs at the kitchen table. "You're something of a mystery. There are no pictures of you in the house, nothing to indicate you'd ever even lived there, except what I found packed away in the attic."

"Mr. Monterey did his best to erase my existence."

"Stephen?"

"Gracious, no. Not Stephen. Colin."

Caroline sank into one of the chairs at the table. "Why doesn't that surprise me?"

Kellen placed pink floral china cups and saucers on the lace tablecloth and a tray with the coffeepot, creamer and sugar bowl.

"Maybe I should start from the beginning," she said, sitting down. She poured coffee into their cups. "Mr. Monterey—Colin—was less than thrilled when Thomas came back from a business trip with me, his new wife, in tow. Tommy and I fell in love the minute we set eyes on each other."

Caroline stirred sugar and cream into her coffee. "Love at first sight? How romantic."

"And it never faded. Those years we had together

were wonderful. Tommy made me laugh. I made him laugh. We were terribly irresponsible, I'm afraid. But we were so young back then.'' Kellen smiled dreamily, then grew solemn. ''Funny, it was only a few years ago, but now it seems like a lifetime has passed.''

''I take it Colin didn't approve of you,'' Caroline said.

''Colin never approved of anything. Such a fussy old man. More concerned about appearances than anything else.'' Kellen sipped her coffee. ''I didn't come with a pedigree. No family lineage dating back hundreds of years, no powerful connections in government or business, no money. I was just an honest young girl, from an honest, hard-working family.''

''And that wasn't good enough for Colin?'' Caroline asked.

''He endured me until…until Tommy died.'' Kellen touched her fingers to her eyes.

Caroline reached across the table and grasped her hand. ''I know this is painful for you. I'm so sorry.''

Kellen gulped down her tears. ''When Tommy died, when I was at my lowest, Colin came to me. He told me I was no longer welcome in his home. He wanted me to leave.''

''That's despicable,'' Caroline said.

''But he told me I shouldn't take Joey with me. He said that Tommy would have wanted his son, a Monterey, raised in the Monterey family with all its power, wealth and privilege.''

''And you went along with him?'' Caroline asked.

"Of course not. I wasn't about to leave my baby behind." Kellen squeezed her eyes shut for a moment. "But Colin kept at me until I believed him. What could I offer Joey? I had no money, no place even to live. How could I take him away from his home, his privileged life-style, and the future that awaited him? Colin convinced me I was being selfish."

"So you left."

"I left." Kellen shook her head. "I was so confused, and so lost without Tommy."

Caroline pushed her coffee cup aside, dreading the question she had to ask. "Did the rest of the family go along with Colin?"

"They didn't know."

"Are you sure? None of them?" Caroline asked. "Not even Stephen?"

"I'm sure Aunt Delfi didn't know," Kellen said. "As for Stephen, I doubt he knew. We never spoke much. He was always busy working. But we had a pleasant relationship. And above all, Stephen wanted Tommy to be happy, and he was happy with me. Stephen had no reason to want me out of the house."

"The law was on your side," Caroline said. "No court in the land would have denied giving you your son."

Kellen uttered a bitter laugh. "I didn't have the kind of money it would take to fight a legal battle with the Montereys."

"Then why didn't you just come back for Joey?"

Caroline asked. ''When you realized what a mistake you'd made, why didn't you go to the house and try to make amends with Colin?''

''I tried,'' Kellen said. ''He refused to let me in, refused to talk to me, refused even to acknowledge my existence. He said he'd have me arrested for trespassing if I came back.''

''But after he died? You could have done it then. No one would have stopped you.''

Kellen sat back in her chair. ''You don't know Stephen Monterey very well.''

Caroline's stomach clenched. ''He wouldn't have kept you from seeing your son.''

''Seeing him? No, he wouldn't have stopped that,'' Kellen said. ''But seeing Joey, visiting with him is not what I wanted. What mother could settle for that? I wanted Joey full-time, in my own home, as my own child. No, Stephen would never have allowed me to take Joey.''

''He might have,'' Caroline said, but in her heart she knew Kellen was right.

''Stephen practically raised Tommy himself. Even though they lived with Colin and had nannies, he looked after Tommy, took care of him, worried about him, watched over him. Stephen would never allow Tommy's son to leave.''

''So you kidnapped him.''

''Yes,'' Kellen said, ''with my brother's help.''

''And Aunt Delfi's,'' Caroline said. ''That was you at the back door, wasn't it? In the green scarf.''

''Delfina didn't agree with what Colin had done.

She wasn't strong enough to stand up to him, but she got around him in her own way. She'd telephone me, sometimes. I'd come to the house and she'd tell me about Joey, how he was doing. I'd watch him play in the yard. She told me about your plans to take him to Westlake Park.''

"Delfina let you into the house last night, didn't she," Caroline said.

Kellen nodded. "She slipped up to the nursery and brought Joey downstairs to us. I left a ransom note thinking the police would believe it was a real kidnapping, and that no one would suspect me. I guess that didn't work.''

"Thanks to me," Caroline said. She would never have suspected Kellen herself if she hadn't stumbled across those letters in the attic that Kellen had written, if she hadn't looked at the ransom note and recognized her handwriting, if she wasn't a graphologist.

Kellen studied her coffee, which had grown cold. "So, Caroline, now that you know the whole story, what are you going to do?''

Caroline sat back in her chair. Good gracious, what was she going to do? She couldn't leave Stephen to worry about his nephew when she knew the child was safe and happy. She couldn't let Brenna go on blaming herself for his disappearance. The police and Pinkerton detectives couldn't waste their time trying to solve a crime where one didn't exist.

How could she tell them Joey was all right without revealing where he was and how she'd gotten the information? Once they knew, they were bound to come after him.

But how could she take a child away from his mother? That wasn't fair to either of them. In fact, it was just plain wrong.

Caroline gazed across the table at Kellen's hopeful face. How had the lives of so many people ended up in her hands?

"Well?" Kellen asked.

"Well..."

A brisk knock sounded on the front door, bringing Kellen up out of her chair.

"Lyle's back already? I didn't realized we'd talked so long. He must have forgotten his key."

Relieved to have a moment to herself, Caroline rose from the table and carried their cups to the sink. What was she going to do? Who would—

"You liar!"

Caroline spun. Kellen stood in the doorway, fists clenched.

"You liar," Kellen said again. "You told me you'd come alone. You said you'd told no one."

"What are you talking about?"

Kellen pointed down the hallway. "Stephen Monterey is on my front porch."

"Stephen?" A cup slipped from the saucer and shattered on the tile floor.

"I won't give him my baby," Kellen swore. "I won't."

"Just calm down," Caroline said, stepping over the broken china. "I don't know how he found me.

I swear, I didn't tell him where I was going. Just let me talk to him. Please, Kellen, stay here and I'll handle Stephen.''

"Can you do that?"

No, probably not, but she couldn't tell Kellen that.

"Just stay here."

Caroline hurried down the hallway, wiping her damp palms against her skirt. She peeked out the window as Kellen must have done, and saw Stephen pacing on the porch. He still wore the trousers and shirt he'd had on this morning. No hat or jacket. He'd followed her.

Pulling in a deep breath, Caroline opened the door. He was in front of her in two long strides, towering over her, glaring at her, angry and confused.

"What the hell are you doing here?" he demanded.

Caroline glanced around. "Please, Stephen, the neighbors."

"I don't give a damn what the neighbors think! I want to know what the hell is going on!"

A vein bulged in his forehead. She'd never seen that before. But she'd never really seen him angry. Stephen prided himself on his self-control.

Caroline stepped back from the door. "Come inside. I'll explain."

He strode into the room, his long strides making the little parlor even smaller.

"Why did you run off like that? If I hadn't seen you leave I'd have thought—I don't know what the hell I would have thought. That you'd been kidnapped, too? That you'd run back to your aunt's? Or maybe Europe?''

"Stephen, I'm so sorry. It didn't occur to me that you'd worry.'' Caroline reached for his arm, but he pulled away.

"What's this all about, Caroline?''

"Joey's safe. He's here.''

Stephen caught her arms and held her, staring into her eyes. "Joey's here? In this house? And he's all right?''

She smiled, seeing the relief in his face. He relaxed his hold on her.

Stephen shook his head. "I don't understand.''

There was no sense in trying to break the news gently. Impossible, under the circumstances. So Caroline just told him straight out.

"Kellen took him. Your Aunt Delfi helped. This is Kellen's home. She wants him back.''

He just stared at her for a moment until the words sunk in. Then he exploded.

"She abandoned him! Walked out! Left him! Then she steals him from me, claiming she wants him back?'' Stephen shook his head. "No. There is no way in hell she's getting that boy away from me.''

Caroline absorbed his anger, then spoke calmly. "She didn't abandon him, Stephen. Your uncle forced her to leave. He wouldn't let her take him.''

"That's a lie. Uncle Colin wouldn't do that.''

"Yes, he would, Stephen. You know it, really, if

you'll just face the truth," Caroline said, keeping her voice even.

Stephen paced a moment, and must have realized she was right because he changed the subject.

"Joey has a good home with me," he said. "He has everything he needs."

"He doesn't have his mother," Caroline said gently.

"Brenna takes care of him."

"But she doesn't love him, Stephen, at least not the way Kellen does. She can't. She's not his mother."

Stephen turned away, pacing, rubbing his neck. "No. He's my brother's child. He belongs in my home. I want him."

"So you can make him part of your collection?"

Stephen rounded on her, glaring. "What the hell are you talking about?"

Her anger stirred. "I'm talking about your music boxes that never play music. Your china figurines that never come out of the cabinet. Your lawn that nobody can walk on. All the perfect little worlds you've created, that you can sit back and look at, and not participate in."

He pulled away, distancing himself from her. "You don't know what you're talking about."

"You've shut yourself off from life, hiding behind your desk and your work. You refuse to feel any emotion." Caroline reached for him, but he pulled away. "See? You won't even let me touch you. You won't accept any comfort."

"I don't need any comfort."

"Yes, you do," Caroline said. "Everybody does. But somehow, trying not to disappoint your uncle and not turn out like your father, you've gotten your emotions all mixed up. You won't allow yourself to feel anything."

"This is nonsense. Where's Joey?" Stephen headed for the staircase in the hallway.

Caroline darted around him and blocked his path. He could easily have pushed her aside, but he stopped.

"You have to listen to reason, Stephen."

"Get out of my way."

He moved around her and went up the stairs.

"Stephen!"

Caroline charged up the steps after him.

Chapter Twenty-One

Caroline caught him in the upstairs hallway. She touched his arm. No match for his strength, she knew he could have kept going. Instead, he stopped.

"Please, Stephen, think about what you're doing. If you take Joey back home with you now, you must ask yourself if this is how you want him to grow up. Living in a house without his parents, without anyone who truly, deeply loves him?"

Stephen stared down at her, the lines of his face grim and unrelenting. His muscles were taut, his breathing heavy.

"Do you really want him to grow up like that?" she asked. "The way you did, Stephen?"

He winced, then let his anger consume him again. "You think you know what I'm like? Just because you take over my house, my life and analyze my handwriting?"

"No," she said softly. "It's because I love you."

Stephen reeled back as if she'd struck him. He

stared at her, vulnerable, stunned. For an instant, Caroline wished the words back, then changed her mind, despite the look on Stephen's face.

Footsteps sounded on the stairs and Kellen joined them in the hallway.

"Please, Stephen," Kellen said gently. "Don't take him away from me. He'll always be your nephew, no matter where he lives. He'll always be Tommy's son, and we both want Joey to know that. I'm going to stay here with my brother, so I can bring Joey to visit as often as you'd like. You're welcome to come here anytime."

Stephen turned away, paced a stride or two in the hallway. He glared at Kellen, then at Caroline for a long, agonizing moment.

Caroline didn't know what he would do, which decision he would make. The lives of so many people hung in the balance at this moment. And again she found herself in the middle of it all.

Finally, Stephen nodded. "He can stay."

Nervous laughter bubbled up in Kellen. "Oh, Stephen, thank you." She reached for him, but he was already going down the stairs.

Caroline went after him. At the foot of the steps she saw him disappear out the front door. Quickly she gathered her cape, hat and handbag from the kitchen and left.

Kellen followed her onto the porch.

"Thank you. For everything," she said, and gave Caroline a hug. "Don't worry. I'll take good care of Joey. Everything will turn out just fine."

Not everything, Caroline thought as she headed toward the train depot.

Stephen was there when she arrived. He stood in the corner, arms folded, aloof and distant. Caroline bought her ticket but didn't approach him.

When the train arrived she sat in the seat beside him. He didn't speak to her, didn't acknowledge her in any way. The trained pulled away from the station. Stephen stared out the window.

The journey back to Los Angeles offered nothing but time for Caroline to sit and think. Here she was beside the man she loved, but she may as well have been on the other side of the world. What was he thinking? she wondered. Was he pondering the things she'd said to him, or had he forgotten already—forgotten her—and retreated into the safety of his world of business decisions.

Maybe she'd gone too far, said things better left unsaid.

She'd always had a propensity for fixing other people's lives, but she'd never felt the urge to take over completely, as she had with Stephen and his family. She'd never been so willing to give of herself before.

It had always been within her, she realized. But it had taken Stephen to bring it out in her. Stephen, and her love for him.

The first night she'd met him she'd sensed the power he could have over her. He'd own her. That's what she'd thought at the time.

Now he did. She was ready and willing to give

herself to him. But did he want her? Caroline would have cried right there on the train if she'd thought it would do any good.

When the train arrived in Los Angeles, they took the trolley from La Grande Station to West Adams Boulevard without speaking, without Stephen so much as looking at her. She'd telephoned from the station in Redlands and left word that Joey had been found safe and well, so the house was empty of detectives when they arrived. Stephen went straight to his office. Caroline, heartsick, went up to her room.

She should check on Brenna, should talk to Delfina, should assure the staff all was well. Should go downstairs and beg Stephen to forgive her for cutting to ribbons the safe little world he'd built for himself. But in the end, Caroline did none of those things.

A long soak in the bath revived her somewhat. She switched on the lamps in her room and dressed in a pale yellow nightgown and robe, and pinned her hair loosely atop her head.

It was dark now, and she could have fallen into bed, pulled the cover over her and not come out again for days. Maybe by then Stephen would have forgiven her, or at least be willing to talk to her.

At any rate, she couldn't stand not knowing what he was thinking, what he was feeling, what he was doing downstairs in his office. If he was angry, she deserved his wrath. If he hated her and never wanted to see her again, she had to know that, too.

Caroline left her room. The house was still. After

what they'd all been through today, everyone needed time to recover.

Descending the stairs, she mentally prepared herself for Stephen's tirade, his hurtful words—anything he might say to her. Possibly she would never see him again after tonight. He might insist that she leave.

Caroline had visions of returning to Aunt Eleanor's house and resuming the husband hunt. Everything in her rebelled. No, she wouldn't go through that again.

She imagined the disappointment on her father's face when she returned to Europe still single. And for the first time, returning to that sort of life didn't seem appealing. Nothing seemed worthwhile without Stephen.

Outside his office, Caroline drew in a deep breath, ready to face whatever might come, then walked inside.

Lamps burned low on the desk and table. Stephen stood at his curio cabinet, his back to her. The doors were open. Music played from all the music boxes, a cacophony of unrecognizable tunes. His prized china figurines sat atop the cabinet, arranged in no particular order. He held one in each hand.

He must have heard her gasp because her bare feet were silent on the floor. He turned and just looked at her for a long time.

Caroline's heart leaped with joy. She could hardly believe her eyes. She squelched the urge to run to him, unable to read in his face how he felt about her now. Stay or go, she couldn't tell.

After a few minutes, Stephen set the figurines aside.

"You missed something significant when you analyzed my handwriting," he said.

"I did?"

He nodded. "The part about how much I hate it when other people are right."

Stephen opened his arms to her, just a tiny bit, and Caroline flew into them. She buried her face in his chest and clutched him tightly. He sealed her against him with an urgent embrace.

"I was afraid you'd hate me," Caroline whispered.

He rubbed his jaw against her hair. "I do hate you. Either that, or it's love. I'm not sure which."

She laughed and turned her face up to his. "Do you think it might be love?"

"I don't know." Stephen strummed his fingers against her cheek. "All these emotions you want me to experience. I can't tell one from the other yet. And they all hurt."

"Well, if it hurts, it's definitely love."

"Just my luck..." Stephen buried his mouth against the hollow of her neck. "Why couldn't it have been just plain old lust?"

"I think there's some of that in there, too," Caroline said, and shifted against him.

Stephen groaned and covered her lips with his. He kissed her deeply until she moaned.

Panting, he broke off their kiss and pressed his forehead against hers. "Caroline, I've wanted you since the night of my birthday party, when I laid eyes on you for the very first time."

She wound her hand around his neck and stroked his hair. "That's lust. I'm sure of it. It was in one of those French books I read."

Stephen groaned again. He pulled in a ragged breath. "But you're the only one I'm lusting after. No other woman will do."

"That's love. I'm pretty sure." She kissed him lightly on the lips.

His mouth devoured hers. Stephen slipped his hand to her waist, then up to cup her breast. She made a little moaning sound and pressed against him.

"Caroline…" His hot breath brushed her mouth. "Caroline…I've never wanted any woman like I want you. I want to show you how much. I want to make you mine."

She opened the top button of his shirt and pressed her palm against his hard chest. Through the fabric of his white undershirt, his muscles twitched. Her knees wobbled.

"I have to leave, Stephen," she whispered.

"What? But…" He loosened his grip on her. "Oh, I—I understand."

Caroline slid her hand deeper inside his shirt and crinkled his chest hair in her fingers.

"I have to go upstairs now," she said, "and match up some neckties."

"But—I—" He realized then what she meant, and swept her off her feet into his arms. "Caroline, Caroline, you're going to make me a raving lunatic."

She giggled and clung to his neck as he carried her up the stairs. He kicked open the door to his bedroom and set her feet on the floor again.

Stephen touched her shoulders and slid his hands down her arms, looking deeply into her eyes. "You're sure?" he asked.

She leaned against him. "I'm sure."

He closed the door and eased away from her to switch on the lamp on the dresser. "I want to see you."

She went into his arms again, feeling lost without them around her. "Do I get to look at you, too?"

"Caroline, honey, you can do whatever you want."

Slowly, she opened all the buttons on his shirt and pulled the suspenders off his shoulders. She tugged the shirt from his trousers. He shrugged out of it and yanked his undershirt over his head.

Caroline smiled at his big bare chest. Dark, crisp hair covered him, tapering to a line that disappeared into his trousers. His belly was tight and hard, like a washboard.

She laid her hands on his shoulders and felt the power in his arms as she slid her fingers downward. Caroline's palms tingled at the feel of him.

Her heart thumped harder in her chest as Stephen pulled the pins from her hair. It fell, curling at her waist. He opened the buttons on her robe. His fingers worked quickly until he pushed the garment back. Heat flamed inside her—from deep within herself, from Stephen, from the warmth of his gaze.

Pushing the robe off her, Stephen looped his arms around her again. He kissed her. Hot, heavy kisses. Caroline rose on her toes, meeting him, wanting him.

Awkwardly, he unbuttoned her nightgown to her waist. Stephen stood back and looked at her, the fabric spread open.

"You're beautiful!" he whispered. Then he swept her into his arms and carried her to the bed. He yanked down the covers and laid her on the cool sheets. Standing over her, he kicked off his shoes, then peeled away his socks and trousers.

Lying on the bed, Caroline watched him. She'd never seen a naked man before, never been naked herself in front of a man. But here, with Stephen, nothing seemed more natural.

He slid out of his underwear and sat on the edge of the bed, bracing himself above her. His heart pumped harder, driving his desire faster and higher. He'd waited for her, for this moment, for weeks, for his whole life. The image before him pressed itself into his mind, sealed there forever. Caroline, her dark hair fanned out over the pillow, her gown open, her sweet body waiting for him.

Stephen stretched out beside her and she came quickly into his arms. He kissed her with a fervor he'd never experienced, something deeper than just a physical reaction.

He dropped his hand to her thigh and raised her nightgown. She trembled at his touch. He shuddered at the sight of her soft flesh. Stephen pulled her gown up until she wiggled out of it, and he flung it across the room.

She came against him fully, her naked body pressed to his. Stephen kissed her, she kissed him. He traced the soft, giving lines of her body. Her thighs, hips, belly, her breasts.

Caroline moaned and moved against him, her own hands finding their way over his body. Stephen groaned with her. He lowered his mouth to sample her breasts, tugging at her sweet nipples. She slid her leg around him, caressing him.

He moved above her, between her thighs, kissing her mouth, her cheek, her neck. He wanted her. He couldn't wait any longer.

She held tightly to him as he eased himself against her. Her hot breath fanned his face. She raised her hips, seeking him.

Stephen fought to hold himself back, to keep from plunging into her. She was small and tight, and that made it even more difficult for him. He kissed her, easing himself into her until her body accepted him.

He moved inside her, creating a whirlpool of emotion she'd never imagined. It stole her breath, made her dizzy. Caroline clung to him as the swirls inside her grew stronger. Faster they came as he moved, urging her on. Her fingers dug into his back. His relentless thrusts drove her higher, higher until they broke inside her. She arched against him, grabbing a handful of his hair as the throbbing peaked, washing over her again and again.

Stephen thought his heart would burst. He pushed himself into her one final time as the exquisite pain rolled through him, out of him, into her. He groaned, his body pulsing with the final strokes of desire. Stephen gathered her into his arms, exhausted and sated.

Some time later, he awoke. The light still burned on the dresser. The pleasant sensation that tingled through him brought a smile to his face.

"Caroline?" He rolled over. She was gone.

Chapter Twenty-Two

"Caroline?"

Stephen untangled himself from the covers and got out of bed. The door to his dressing room was open. Light spilled into the bedroom.

Rubbing his eyes, he crossed the room and found Caroline inside. His heart tumbled. She wore his white shirt, sleeves rolled back, the tail flirting with her thighs.

He leaned against the door casing. "What are you doing?"

She spun around. Her cheeks glowed and her hair was mussed. Beautiful.

Caroline waved her hand toward the rows of his suits, hanging in perfect order. Dozens of them, with white shirts alongside, neckties hung in perfect symmetry.

She touched her finger to her lips, studying his wardrobe. "I've never seen a man's dressing room before," she said. Then she looked at him standing naked in the doorway. "I've seen several new things tonight."

He came to her in the center of the room. "You're pleased, I hope, with all your new experiences?"

She grinned. "All very…impressive."

Stephen slid his arms around her. "Come back to bed."

"I can't just now," Caroline said. "I need to take care of your neckties. After all, that's what I'm up here for, isn't it?"

"That is definitely not what you're up here for," he said.

Caroline batted her lashes innocently at him. "Then why am I here?"

Stephen laughed low in his throat, his desire for her blooming all over again. "Let me show you."

He carried her back to bed and snuggled under the covers with her. He kissed her, touched her everywhere he'd wanted to earlier but hadn't managed to before being overcome by more urgent needs.

Caroline did the same. With curiosity, gentleness, boldness she acquainted herself with him. She found the most delightful places on his body, places that made him writhe, made him moan, made him do the same to her.

They made love again in what began as an exchange of pleasure but ended up frantic and urgent. Caroline rose to a peak and he followed quickly, before collapsing into each other's arms.

Afterward, Stephen propped himself up on his elbow and gazed down at her. He traced his finger down her face, over her breasts to her belly.

"You're the most beautiful woman I've ever known," he said.

Caroline rubbed her hand across his chest. "Those French books. The diagrams didn't do the male body justice."

He grinned, pleased. "You really read such books?"

"Of course."

He closed his eyes. "Oh, Caroline..." Stephen leaned forward and muzzled his nose against her neck. "When you say things like that I—"

She slid her hand downward and captured him with her palm. "According to the book, this isn't supposed to keep happening."

Stephen lifted his head. "It's all right with you, though?"

She smiled. "Let me show you how happy it makes me. Maybe I'll tell you about some of the diagrams I saw."

He shifted above her. "Oh, Caroline..."

When Stephen woke the next time, it was still dark and Caroline was still beside him. He watched her for a long time, studying each feature, committing it to memory.

It was one thing to see her in his office every day downstairs, dressed properly, quite another to have her asleep in his bed, mussed and tousled from their lovemaking. Both pictures were worthy of a lifetime of remembering.

All this business of experiencing his emotions she'd talked to him about—of not hiding behind his desk and his work—made sense to him. He hadn't known he was doing it until she'd pointed it out.

He wasn't sure he liked it, though. It hurt. But with Caroline it was a pleasurable hurt.

Stephen didn't know if he could change in the way she wanted him to. He'd lived his life for a long time as he was. But he'd try.

The one thing he was certain of was that he couldn't live without Caroline.

She roused from her light sleep a few minutes later and smiled as soon as she opened her eyes. Stephen's heart thumped a little harder.

He rolled out of bed. "Come with me."

Caroline pushed her hair off her shoulder. "We're going somewhere?"

"Come on." Stephen hunted around the room until he found his drawers and trousers, and pulled them on.

"What are you up to?" she asked, grinning.

He caught her hand and pulled her to her feet, sighing longingly at the sight of her naked body. "I really hate to do this, but…" He dropped her nightgown over her head.

"Stephen, what on earth is going on?" she asked, closing the buttons.

"Don't act so surprised," he said. "It was your idea."

"My idea?" Caroline reached for her robe, but he shook his head.

"Just as you are." Stephen took her hand and led her out of his room.

Being the middle of the night, it was unlikely anyone in the house would be up and about, but still Caroline felt a little strange walking the halls in only her nightgown, with her hair loose around her shoulders, and Stephen beside her dressed only in his trousers. She went with him, though, willing and a little curious.

They went downstairs and out the back entrance of the house. Stephen stopped on the porch, still holding her hand.

Faint light from the moon lit the lawn. The night was cool and crisp. Flowers from the garden scented the air.

Stephen walked down the steps and onto the lawn. He stopped and looked down at his feet. He wiggled his toes, shifted from one foot to the other, testing the feel of the cool grass.

"Well, I don't know," he said thoughtfully. "I suppose it has its merits."

Caroline smiled and slid her arm around his waist, remembering that it had indeed been her idea to run barefoot across the lawn. She looked down at her own feet.

"I like it," she said.

Hand in hand they strolled through the grass, soaking in the silence, the chill of the dew, the warmth of their entwined fingers.

At the fountain, Stephen sat down on the marble edge of the bottom tier and rolled up his pant legs. He stuck his toe into the water.

He sucked in a quick breath. "Cold."

Caroline sat down beside him and gathered her nightgown up to her thighs. They looked at each other, then both stuck their legs in up to their knees.

Both gasped at the cool water. Caroline shuddered and snuggled against him. Stephen circled his arm around her.

They sat together for a long time, swishing their feet, leaning their heads against one another.

"It was good of you to leave Joey with Kellen," Caroline said.

"He belongs with his mother, as you said. But I'll miss him."

"Kellen won't keep him from you. In fact, in time she might even move back here."

"I could see that happening," he agreed.

"You ought to look into investing in her brother's orange groves. They're quite profitable."

"Richard and Brenna really are in love with each other. I realized it when Joey was kidnapped." Stephen kissed the top of Caroline's head. "Don't you get tired of being right all the time?"

"It wears me out."

Stephen chuckled and kissed her again. "Any more observations?"

"Well," Caroline said, "I know how to solve your Johannesburg problem."

"All right, let's hear it."

She looked up at him. "Send Richard to replace Girard."

"Richard?"

"Yes, he's perfect for the job. He knows your business inside out. And you can trust him, Stephen, you know you can."

"But he'll need money to establish himself there. Richard can't afford that."

"Then give him some money," Caroline said. "Call it a bonus or something. You'll get it back ten times over in profits, and peace of mind."

Stephen grunted.

"And that way, he and Brenna can get married."

Stephen chuckled. "That's what's really behind this whole idea of yours, isn't it?"

"Things will be different for them in Johannesburg. It's not like society here in Los Angeles, or New York, or San Francisco. And with Richard there to take over your holdings, he'll have instant credibility, regardless of Brenna's background."

"And what am I supposed to do for an assistant if Richard leaves?" Stephen asked.

"That's simple," Caroline said. "I'll be your assistant."

"Ha!" Stephen laughed. "That will never work."

She chucked him on the arm. "Why not? I'd make an excellent assistant."

"It wouldn't work because I'd never get one damn thing done. I'd be chasing you around the office all day. We'd end up penniless, living on the street, destitute."

"Stephen, you're being silly."

He touched his finger to her chin and tilted her face up to his. "I don't want you to be my assistant, Caroline. I want you to be my wife."

She gasped. "Your—wife?"

Stephen caught her hand and pressed her palm against his chest. "Can you look into my heart and see what's written there, Caroline? I love you."

He pulled her into his embrace and she came against him, smiling and happy.

"I love you," Stephen said again.

Caroline leaned back, looking up at him. "Are you sure, Stephen? It's love and not just lust?"

He grinned. "I'm sure I'll be lusting after you for the rest of my life, married or not. But I do love you, Caroline. I'm sure it's love. So, will you marry me?"

"Oh, yes."

She tried to go into his arms again, but Stephen held back. "Only a few weeks ago you didn't want to get married. Are you sure this is what you want?"

"I'm very sure."

They kissed, then Stephen pulled away. He frowned slightly.

"We'll probably have children, won't we?" he said.

"If things keep going the way they have tonight, we'll have one soon." Caroline took his hand. "Is that all right with you?"

He nodded thoughtfully. "It may take a while for me to get used to the idea. I don't want to be a father to our child the way I was an uncle to Joey. I want to be more involved. But I'm not really sure how to go about that.''

"We'll start slowly," Caroline said. "One baby at a time."

"I think I can handle that." Stephen kissed her again. "I can do anything with you, Caroline."

That afternoon Stephen sat at his desk in his office, trying to work. He might really end up penniless, he mused, pushing away the report in front of him, because he really couldn't keep his mind on his work. Caroline, of course, occupied his thoughts. Caroline and their night together.

She'd taken it into her head to go shopping this afternoon, otherwise he'd still be upstairs in bed with her right now. He needed to be. Stephen shifted in his chair. Even after last night, he hadn't gotten enough of her.

A little commotion drifted down the hallway and Stephen sprang from his desk, hoping it was Caroline returning. He hurried to the doorway, not caring if he looked anxious or excited. He saw her in the vestibule removing her hat, directing the driver to carry her packages into the house.

Stephen folded his arms and watched her walk toward him. She had on a pink shirtwaist with a big bow at her throat. He couldn't wait to take it off of her.

"I missed you," he said, as she came into the office.

She paused in the doorway and stretched up to kiss his lips. He caught her waist and pulled her close, kissing her and sighing heavily.

"I bought you something," she said, pulling away and walking to his desk.

He followed her like a little puppy, and didn't care. "Neckties more to your liking?" he asked.

She smiled knowingly. "Not neckties, but something I hope you'll like even better."

Stephen latched on to her waist and pulled her against him. "Show me now."

"Not so fast." She grinned and walked her fingers up his jacket. "Did you talk to Richard while I was gone?"

"I did. And after he got over the shock, he agreed to take the Johannesburg position."

"That's wonderful." She stroked her fingers over his chest. "Did he tell Brenna?"

"I'm pretty sure that right now they're upstairs rolling around in her bed, celebrating their upcoming nuptials."

Her eyes widened. "Oh, Stephen. They're upstairs in bed?"

"Does that shock you?"

"No, I just wish it were us."

"Oh, Caroline..." Stephen pulled her against him and laid claim to her mouth with a hot, wet kiss.

Intrusive throat clearing came from across the room. "Excuse me, Mr. Monterey."

Stephen growled and released her. Charles stood in the doorway.

"You have a visitor, sir. Mr. Russell Pickette."

"Pickette?" Stephen moved away from Caroline, his playful mood gone.

"Shall I tell him you're not available, sir?" Charles asked.

Stephen glared at the butler for a moment. "Send him in."

When Charles disappeared, Caroline went to Stephen. "I looked at those documents and—"

"Don't worry," he said. "I'll handle Pickette."

"But Stephen—"

He held up his hand for silence. A moment later, Russell Pickette came into the office holding his battered hat, but standing straight and proud. He nodded politely to Caroline, then turned to Stephen.

"You come to a decision yet, Mr. Monterey?" he asked.

Stephen studied him for a moment, then walked to his desk and took out the land contract. He glanced over it, tapped it against his palm, then presented it to Russell Pickette.

"This document is authentic," Stephen said.

Pickette's eyes widened as he looked down at the papers in his hand. "Well, thank you, Mr. Monterey."

"I'll have my lawyers complete the transfer tomorrow."

"Thank you kindly, sir. Thank you." Pickette offered his hand. Stephen shook, sealing their deal, and Pickette left the office.

"Stephen, are you sure?" Caroline asked.

"I'm sure. Pickette should tend to the farm he's built, raise his children, enjoy his life," Stephen said. "Because that's what I'm going to do."

Caroline went into his arms, pleased that he'd made the right decision without knowing what she knew—that the document was genuine.

"You continue to surprise me," she said.

Stephen grinned and kissed her neck. "Can we go upstairs now?"

She pushed him away. "Not yet. I want to give you the gift I bought you in town first."

He fidgeted. "All right."

Caroline left the office, then returned a moment later with a huge box wrapped in white paper and tied with a red bow. She set it down on his desk.

"I was thinking of all the years that have passed already," Caroline said. "Special occasions in your life that I missed. You just had your birthday and I didn't get you anything. So I bought you a gift."

Stephen raised an eyebrow at her, then at the box. He pulled loose the ribbon, ripped away the paper and pried off the lid.

"Oh my God…" he wheezed.

Stephen reached into the box and pulled out a pair of ladies' high buttoned shoes and a wide-brimmed hat trimmed with ribbons and an ostrich feather.

"Happy birthday," Caroline said, and took the hat and shoes from him. "Lock the door, Stephen, and clear off your desk."

* * * * *

If you enjoyed what you just read,
then we've got an offer you can't resist!

Take 2 bestselling love stories FREE!

Plus get a FREE surprise gift!

TAKE A TRIP ACROSS AMERICA FROM SEA TO SHINING SEA WITH THESE HEARTFELT WESTERNS FROM

Harlequin® Historical

In March 2000, look for

THE BONNY BRIDE by **Deborah Hale**
(Nova Scotia, 1814)

and

ONCE A HERO by **Theresa Michaels**
(Arizona & New Mexico, 1893)

In April 2000, look for

THE MARRYING MAN by **Millie Criswell**
(West Virginia, 1800s)

and

HUNTER'S LAW by **Pat Tracy**
(Colorado, 1880s)

Harlequin Historicals
The way the past *should* have been.

Available at your favorite retail outlet.

HARLEQUIN®
Makes any time special ™

Back by popular demand are

DEBBIE MACOMBER's

Hard Luck, Alaska, is a
town that needs women!
And the O'Halloran brothers
are just the fellows
to fly them in.

Starting in March 2000 this beloved series returns
in special 2-in-1 collector's editions:

MAIL-ORDER MARRIAGES, featuring
Brides for Brothers and *The Marriage Risk*
On sale March 2000

FAMILY MEN, featuring
Daddy's Little Helper and *Because of the Baby*
On sale July 2000

THE LAST TWO BACHELORS, featuring
Falling for Him and *Ending in Marriage*
On sale August 2000

Collect and enjoy each MIDNIGHT SONS story!

Available at your favorite retail outlet.

HARLEQUIN®
Makes any time special ™

Harlequin® Historical

is proud to offer four very different
Western romances that will
warm your hearts....

In January 2000, look for
THE BACHELOR TAX
by **Carolyn Davidson**
and
THE OUTLAW'S BRIDE
by **Liz Ireland**

In February 2000, look for
WRITTEN IN THE HEART
by **Judith Stacy**
and
A BRIDE FOR McCAIN
by **Mary Burton**

Harlequin Historicals
The way the past *should* have been.

Available at your favorite retail outlet.

HARLEQUIN®
Makes any time special™

Visit us at www.romance.net

HHWEST6

COMING NEXT MONTH FROM

HARLEQUIN HISTORICALS